# POEMS AND MONSTERS

## Adam Davies

# Acknowledgements

I want to thank Gwendolynn Guthrie for both her excellent artwork and for her diligence in formatting and downloading this book. It has been difficult to write, but I'm glad I did it. And I really hope you enjoy it.

# CHAPTER ONE

## The Disappeared

The journey down had been uneventful for all of them. Rick was ever so confident that they were going to have an encounter. Rick was confident about everything though. It was his nature. He always had been. Mike, on the other hand, was by his own admission, a pretty nervous guy. It had taken a lot of courage for him to do this, to stand up to Maisy, his wife. She had never liked Rick. She didn't trust him at all. Mike had accepted this. He had bit his lip. Held in his anger and frustration, like he did about all the things that Maisy said which upset him. This time though, she had cost him dear. In order to really be admitted into the `Inner Circle`, as Rick called it, you really had to have your partner come along too. Maisy would never agree to that. Ian had been admitted without a partner that was certainly true. In fact, people said that that Ian had never had a girlfriend in as long as they had known him. Ian was special though. For he had skills, special skills, which Rick needed. Rick didn't particularly need Mike for anything. Mike knew that. And it troubled him.

The last part of the drive was at best tricky, and at worst perilous. They had turned off the main road now, and were just on dirt logging roads. They weaved for miles and miles, twisting their way further into the forest. Sometimes the branches hit the truck, which made Mike duck on instinct. They must be ruining Rick's paintwork, thought Mike, as he heard yet another branch scratch against its side, screeching as it did so.

In fact, the nearer they got, the happier Rick got. Now he was whistling, and sometimes even singing! "We will be there soon now gentlemen! Don't you worry!" Said Rick in his booming voice. Rick was a big man. He stood at 6 feet 8 inches, and even in the car he dwarfed over Mike, who's slight five feet six inch frame, made them almost appear like father and son, rather than what they actually were, two middle aged men.

Ian sat in the back, saying nothing, as usual. That wasn't awkward though, as Rick always did enough talking for all three of them combined.

Mike winced as the wheels of the truck pushed against a drop hundreds of feet into the trees below. He didn't want to show any weakness in front of Rick though, so he tried to hide his fear as best he could. He did his normal trick of biting his lip, to try to keep calm.

"Aha! We are here Gentlemen!" said Rick. Now, remember my instructions please. Absolutely no talking whatsoever until I have made the special announcement, understood?"

"Understood," said Mike and Ian in sync. They followed Rick out of the car and did exactly what Rick had instructed them to do the night before when he had briefed them at the house once again, and made them sign the special contract.

They stood in a straight line now, Ian and he both flanked Rick, who stood in the middle. Rick was holding the sacred hand bell.

Now he began to speak "Brothers! Sisters! Please know that we come here to honor you! We come here in the name of friendship, and of peace!"

Then Rick used the hand bell and rang it so that it chimed three times. And only three. He had been told by them that this was a signal that they should follow. That they understood that this was his signal to show that he had arrived. One day, impostors pretending to be Rick might come, and might shout too. Only Rick though, and those he brought with him, would understand the special signal. That was just for them.

Now Rick began to mumble something and started swaying as he did so. Mike understood that this was the `special language` that they spoke to each other in. Rick had told them that most of the time they communicated with him in a form of telepathy, but as he was their chosen ambassador, he had been allowed to learn some of their `special language ` too. Mike stood waiting, scanning the bushes, but there was nothing. He looked across at Rick, whose whole body seemed tense now. In contrast, Ian hadn't moved at all.

Then Rick suddenly relaxed and smiled. Then he said. "All is good my brothers. We have been given permission to stay. As it is getting late now, I think we must unpack and get everything ready. As you know, it all needs to be in place before dark. For we cannot leave `The Circle` after that."

The circle Rick was referring to, Mike thought, was perfect. An exact circle about 30 feet round by 30 feet in diameter. At one side of it, there was a small path, which led into woods which were now getting increasingly gloomier, as the light failed. On the other side, was the dirt track on which they had just come in. Mike wasn't used to camping, and now he found himself on a hillside, miles from any other human.

Ian's face had been implacable on the way up. He had sat in the back of the vehicle and had barely spoken. Now though, he almost seemed like a different person. He was happy, animated, and he and Rick could barely stop talking. Their tone seemed a bit strange to Mike though, and he wasn't sure why. It almost seemed like they were speaking slowly. Why though? What could that mean. Was he just imagining it?

After all, he was very tired. He shook his head. He was nervous, and his imagination must be getting the better of him, he thought to himself.

They quickly unpacked the cots and laid some blankets on them. There were no tents, Rick always apparently insisted on that. In order to build trust, the creatures needed to see them, that was important, he said. Even after years with Rick they were still shy, and they needed that reassurance apparently.

Mike could relate to that shyness very well. He hoped that the creatures would come in. Rick said that it was a great honor for him if they did so. In order for it to happen though, they must be sleeping. Rick said they would only come in then, and that it was really the most important thing. In fact, apart from the confidentiality of the area, it was an absolute imperative. Rick had kept emphasizing this to them during dinner last night. Kept on going on about it, until 3 am in fact. Then they had set off for the 7 hour drive at 6am. Mike was exhausted. Both he and Ian had offered to drive, but Rick had declined. "Nobody drives my truck, except for me, gentlemen," said Rick, chuckling as he said so. Rick seemed to chuckle at himself a lot, thought Mike.

They walked a short distance into the woods, and put the gifting bowls down in the specially arranged place. Not too far into the woods, but far enough so that they could not be seen from the camp. Each of the three bowls was brimming with food, food that Rick said the creatures liked. Sweet things mostly. Stuff high in calories. Maybe they needed the energy, thought Mike.

By the time they returned to the cots, it was almost dark. Rick had forbidden them to leave *The Circle* after that, so there was little else to do but go to bed now.

Their cots had been placed in a straight line. Rick was on the side nearest where the truck was parked, and Mike had the middle cot. They were spaced less than a few feet apart, but even so, Mike was glad he did not have the end cot, like Ian, which was closest to the woods.

Rick played some soothing music. A sort of melancholic sax. Rick explained that `they` liked it. Mike was anxious still though. He had wanted to see one his whole life. Since he was a boy. He was in his late forties now. Would this be the time? Rick seemed to think it would be. They were here for four nights before they had to return. There was time.

He lay there just looking up at the stars, listening to the music. Nobody spoke now, not even Rick. Mike quietly preyed to see one, and then he waited. Rick had clicked the music off by now, and after only a few minutes, he could hear both Rick and Ian breathing heavily. Attached to the top of the truck, was a parabolic dish. Rick would spend hours after that going through the recordings, listening for evidence of them coming into camp. And for any language they spoke. Particularly that, so he could post it in the group for the rest of the followers. There were a few hundred devotees now, and they all anxiously awaited updates. They all wanted to be here, some would have given all that they own just to swap places with him right now, Mike knew that. He was really surprised that he had been selected. He was determined not to let Rick down. All he had to do was go to sleep….

Mike closed his eyes and waited. He tried to emulate the breathing of the others and began synchronizing his breath with Ian's. This would help him relax, surely.

It was at that point that he felt the worse pain in his entire life. Something had hold of his ankle, and he opened his eyes wide at the shock and agony of it. Looming above him was the most hideous creature he had ever seen! It had the head of a dog, with small red eyes. Although it was difficult to tell in the dark, it seemed to be even bigger than Rick. So many teeth thrust out from its jaw, at strange almost impossible angles, and it's now ever widening mouth began to curl into a snarl.

Mike tried to get up, to move to shout, anything! He could only move his head, and he turned it furiously from side to side, desperately trying to contact Rick and Ian in any way he could now, as the creature was seemingly going in for the kill.

What was this thing? This wasn't one of them, the wonderful creatures of this sacred place! This thing was going to kill him! Eat him, and –

Then Mike's whole body relaxed. He closed his eyes and the pain just evaporated. He had never known such bliss. He was sleeping now. He was healing. He was strong now.

## Chapter Two

### 1978

Isabella knew she was supposed to stay with Jake, but this was so much fun! Even better than the picnic. She was supposed to stay with her brother and play near him, never to go out of his sight. This was so much more fun though! She had to go! These little men and women, how they danced, how they twirled! The two little men were so funny, they made her giggle! Both of them were dressed really oddly. Both had similar outfits on. They wore green tunics, tights, and wooden shoes. They were even physically similar, with conical pointed hats on. However, there was one important difference. One had a blue hat, and one a red. They were only really small, only six inches tall she guessed, but even so, they were making such a noise with all their singing and dancing, that she was amazed that Jake her brother, and her Mum and Dad, could not at least hear them. Seeing them might be another matter, because she understood that the grass in the meadow was very long, and that these little creatures could easily remain hidden within it.

She heard the fairies call to her first! Their voices were so pretty! High pitched and undulating, it sounded to Isabella like they were singing, even when they were just speaking.

"Isabella! Isabella! Come and join the dance, won't you join us, won't you join us, come and join the dance?" The fairies had sung to her. Isabella recognized them as fairies from her books. She loved reading, and at aged seven and a half, the half being very important let me tell you, she could read very easily on her own. Jake, and Mum and Dad were busy kicking a soccer ball around, and she didn't like that game at all. So, she had stayed to play with Mandy, her dolly. Mandy had pigtails, with blue ribbons in her hair, to match her blue dress, just like Isabella.

She liked to imagine Mandy was real, a real little person. Isabella was at school now, but the other boys and girls were not really like her. They were stupid, they couldn't read or write anything like as well as her, and their conversation, such as it was, was stupid really. So, there was Jake and Mum and Dad. Jake was much bigger than her though, and he was a boy. Mum and Dad were, well, doing what Mum's and Dad's do. They both had read her stories at bedtime though, and she always enjoyed that. Thus, she was well familiar with the escapades of the fairies! Now, here were some right in front of her! She ran to the little clearing by an old tree, when she saw them dancing.

The fairies were moving so swiftly now, she could just about make out their shapes. They were just like the illustrations she had seen, they were very pretty with tiny wings, and lovely shimmering silver dresses. They spun and twirled together, as they did so, little bells seemed to chime, and they laughed and laughed.

The little gnomes, for that is what they truly were, were doing a sort of little jig, round and round they went, round and round. In fact, they went so fast that they made just one silver blur. The gnomes were slower, but they too seemed to be having a great time, and they both began whistling.

By now, Isabella had arrived at the little grass circle, and both excited and astonished at what she saw, she began shouting.

"Mum! Dad! Jake!!! Get here quick! Fairies and Gnomes! Fairies and Gnomes! They are dancing together! It's amazing! Come and see!! Quick quick, come and see!"

Isabella was now turned in the direction of her parents and brother, who although they were less than thirty yards away, seemed unable to hear her, even when she was shouting. This confused her, but she did not have time to react, because then one of the fairies spoke directly to her.

"Hello Isabella! " Said the first silver fairly, "I am Daisy, and this is Bluebell." . With this, the fairies both curtsied to Isabella.

"Hello Isabella!" Said the Gnome with the red hat. "I am Bumble and this is Stiffle. " With this, they both bowed to Isabella.

"Your Mum and Dad and brother can't hear you yet, "said Daisy, "but if they do, that will make us disappear, and you don't want that do you?"

"Oh no, "said Isabella. "I don't want that, you look like you are having such fun!"

"Yes we are, "said Bumble, "Would you like to join us, we are going to have a FEAST!"

"Oh yes!" Said Isabella, who by now was very hungry.

"Excellent!" Said Bumble, "all you have to do is say, "I would like to join the good folk! Three times, and you can! It must be no more than three times, or it won't work. Can you say it for us now, Isabella?" Said Bumble.

"Yes, no more than three times," said Daisy. "You must be very careful and JUST say, "I would like to join the good folk. Have you got it, Isabella?"

"Yes, I understand", Isabella replied.

"Excellent!" laughed Daisy.

With that, Isabella closed her eyes and said:

"I would like to join the good folk!

I would like to join the good folk!

I would like to join the good folk!"

When she opened her eyes, a giant Mandy doll was by her side. And she was in a forest, no wait! There were the fairies and the gnomes in front of her! She had shrunk to their size. In fact, she was actually a little smaller than them now. She could make out their features more clearly now, and could see that the Gnomes were older men, and the Fairies young women. Now she was small, and in front of four strange adults, she began to hesitate and look around.

Daisy then grabbed her hand, and Isabella felt a tingling in that hand as she did so. Then Daisy spoke kindly, to her "don't worry. We have a feast prepared! Come and see, Isabella! Come and see!" She and Bluebell giggled as she said this, and they danced towards a little green door in the tree, gently pulling Isabella with them as they did so. Bumble and Stiffle followed directly behind them.

Daisy pushed the door open, and right inside was a sunlit meadow like the one she had just been in. Except in this one, sat an enormous table, groaning with food. On it was every type of food she liked. Coconut pie, and lemonade, chocolate and peanut and jelly sandwiches!

There were five chairs at the table. Daisy took Isabella directly to the one at the head of the table and motioned her to sit down.

Then, she and Bluebell, sat down in the carved wooden chairs on either side of the table, while Stiffle poured her a drink of lemonade.

After she had sat down, Bumble smiled at her and said, "what would you like to eat, Isabella?"

Isabella looked in awe at the choices before her "I will have the coconut cream pie!" She declared.

The Fairies and the Gnomes all laughed in joy and Bumble said "excellent choice!"

He then cut her a great big piece, and handed it to her on a silver plate, on which rested a silver fork.

"However will I finish this?" Thought Isabella. Then her stomach rumbled, and she knew how and why. She put the pie in her mouth and started to chew. It tasted so so delicious! She swallowed it.

"Why this pie is the best pie I have ever tasted in the whole world!" Said Isabella to Daisy.

As soon as she said this, the little door in the tree slammed shut…

Jake called out for his sister once again. His throat was hurting now "Isabella! Isabella!" He listened. On either side of him, his mother and father were doing the same, their voices increasing in both pitch and desperation, just like him.

Jake looked around. He could see nothing around him except the meadow and within it, a little flattened circle of grass. He stopped to pick up Isabella's doll, Mandy which was within it.

"Isabella! Isabella! I have found Mandy! I know you lost her, but she is here! Isabella! Isabella!"

Isabella never replied.

### Five Years Ago:

Zak Halliday had had enough. Not just of his job in cyber security, which he was actually very good at, but of the pressures of life. He was just 28, and already he had an apartment that even those other six figure professionals in San Francisco would envy. He had all that he wanted. A really hot girlfriend who adored him. He was trim and good looking. He had it all. When he was 13, and the geeky kid who everyone bullied, he had longed for all that he now had. Then he grew and through intelligence and quick wits, he had achieved success. He would be a millionaire before the age of 30. He could do anything.

Yet Zak was not satisfied. He wasn't satisfied and he didn't know why he wasn't. And for that, he was disgusted with himself. It wasn't that he was an arrogant man you see, quite the reverse in fact. He was grateful for all that had been given to him, even though it was mostly through his own hard work and ability that he had got it.

Which is why he felt bad? And then he felt worse for feeling bad. He just couldn't process his ingratitude. He just couldn't say what was wrong. So, he had decided to spend a few days out hiking in Yosemite to try and clear his head. He didn't want to use therapists. He wanted fresh air and nature that would bring him back he reasoned. Make him happy.

He had rented a cabin on the outskirts of the area, and drove to some well-worn trails. He enjoyed the outdoors, but in truth, he felt more comfortable in an office, then the woods. Ever the planner, he had a comprehensive kit in his daypack. This included maps, a med kit, plenty of food and water, and a bear spray just in case. Today, he would be following an 8 mile loop trail, with pretty clear directions. In addition to this, every 800 yards or so, there were very clear markers on the trail, so he couldn't get lost. It was a gorgeous sunny day, and Zak actually felt really happy for the first time in ages. The sun was shining, and as he drew in breath on that crisp April morning, he finally felt connected with nature and happy. He could smell the pine trees, and how clean and pure everything seemed. Maybe this was the real life for him. Maybe he could train to be a Ranger? It would be a massive drop in income of course, but he didn't care. He didn't have children to support. Not yet, anyway. Maybe in the future though? Then, Zak's thoughts of his future were suddenly halted. For just 10 yards off the trail, was a carved wooden staircase! Just a staircase, and a handrail. Zak reckoned that there were about twenty steps on it. It seemed old and ornate. Yet there was no structure to support it. No signs, nothing.

Was it some piece of modern art? Zak wondered? He had bought a few pieces recently as part of his portfolio, but if it was, then the artist was very foolish. For, as he approached it, he could see that it was carved mahogany. Antique wood and very expensive. Yet, exposed to the elements out here, it was surely going to get badly damaged very quickly. Zak smiled to himself, and decided he would go up it, just for fun. After all, he wasn't in a rush, and this thing was certainly strange and cool. When he got to the top, Zak took a second to look around at the view. Then he vanished. Just like that!

    The professionals searched very hard for Zak. Even the dogs couldn't pick up his scent. It seemed to just stop a little off trail. The expensive private detectives his parent's hired couldn't find anything either. Eventually, all of them were forced to conclude that Zak was gone for good…


## Two Years Ago

    Jake had looked all around the tree. It was weird. When Marybelle had first contacted him to say that there was a Bigfoot living under a tree and that she spoke to him and knew where he was, he had dismissed it as nonsense. He got all sort of requests all the time from people to come and look at their evidence. For example, he had been sent many pictures of bushes with red circles in them. These were generally from well - meaning people, but there was no Bigfoot in them, they were just empty bushes. He had become something of an officiant in paredolia, the wishful desire to see faces and shapes where none exists. He had never seen a Bigfoot in any of them though, and nor did he expect to. And by now he had seen hundreds. So, the notion of flying across the country to look at Marybelle's `magic tree` was preposterous really. So why was he so drawn to this ridiculous story?

He had persuaded his friends Simon and Philip to join him. They were a little reluctant at first, but eventually they had agreed as they were going to do an investigation in the Cascades anyway, and seven nights in the area wouldn't do any harm.

Yet when they had turned up, there was *something* there. When Marybelle spoke to whatever was there, and stamped her foot, it knocked back. When he stamped his foot, it also responded in kind. It seemed particularly fond of the gifts she gave it. Sometimes food like apples, and sometimes little trinkets like glass baubles. Jake might have dismissed it as nothing more than a knocking tree branch, yet he had heard it growl and even laugh on one occasion!

He had also noticed something else that disturbed him. When his friends Simon and Philip were around the tree, even for only a few minutes, their personalities *changed,* they became more aggressive and cantankerous. Was it just a coincidence? How could any creature actually understand English? It just did not seem remotely plausible, and yet there it was.

They had carried out as thorough survey as they could during their short stay, using the latest technology, including thermal imaging cameras, but nothing had showed up, and they could find no entrances to any den the creature might have, no passageway or trails of any kind. He had left perplexed. Jake had left Marybelle with some trail cameras to continue her research after he departed for New York. Although the `offerings` continued to disappear, and the creature continued to respond to Marybelle, no pictures were ever captured on the cameras.

Jake was perplexed.

# Chapter Three

## Present Day Oregon

Barbara Ellis struggled as she got out of Rick's jeep. For her now, there was almost constant pain. At first, she had felt just really really tired. Then she had started to feel sick. She knew something was seriously wrong even before she went to the Doctor's. So, when she and her husband David finally did go , it came as no surprise to find out she had what was almost nonchalantly referred to as 'stage 3B uterine cancer.` The operation to remove it had happened just a few weeks afterwards. It had taken six hours; in fact the surgeon's hands had turned blue from working so hard to remove the cancer. At first, it had seemed like an amazing success. All of that horrible growth inside her, had been removed. Then the chemotherapy had started. The beautiful long blonde hair that she had so loved had fallen out in big chunks. David had told her that "it would all grow back," and of course she had believed him. It should have been true. Except it wasn't. The bone pain from the treatments continued, but it never helped. Her immune system crashed. Then the cancer came back. It had spread through her pelvis. It was stage four. And now the Doctor's told her she had just weeks to live.

She had loved David for over thirty years. He was a wonderful man. A good father, a loyal husband. She had known he had had an interest in Bigfoot's all his life. He and his friends had even gone on the odd weekend looking for them. Without any success of course. That's because they don't exist, thought Barbara to herself. So, when David told him about this guy Rick, who said that magical healing Bigfoots could work their special powers and heal her, she had laughed. David had seemed hurt at this though. Nothing had worked, so why not give this a try? Just one night. What did they have to lose? Rick charged four hundred bucks a night, per person, but they were rich, so that would be nothing to them. Or rather, nothing to David, once she was gone.

So here she found herself, in the middle of nowhere Oregon, with this snake oil salesman, and her beloved husband.

She disliked Rick the moment she met him. Even though he was charming to her. There was something `off` about him. She couldn't put her finger on what it was, but she knew it was there. David really liked him though. And if this helped that wonderful man, then she would indulge him. She knew she would be gone soon, and he needed to feel he had tried everything to save her. So, she indulged him, and was polite to Rick.

Barbara watched from the Truck, as Rick went through some bizarre ritual ringing a hand bell and announcing their arrival to the empty woods. When Rick had asked the Bigfoots to heal her, it was all she could do to stop herself from laughing out loud!

She was stiff from the journey, and both David and Rick had to almost carry her to the cot that was placed nearest to the truck for her. She took her meds, this time to knock herself out, as she wanted to indulge Rick with only the minimum of her conversation.

She felt a sharp pain during the night, which caused her to jolt slightly, but then she went into a really deep sleep, and forgot all about it.

The next morning, she was awake before either Rick or her husband. She opened her eyes, and blinked up at her forest. Rick and her husband were lying still. She moved her legs. Then her arms freely. She felt no pain. Maybe her meds were still working, she thought to herself. Then she got up and walked! Walked for the first time in a year, properly and without pain!

Oh, maybe I am just dreaming. "David, David! Barbara shouted, "watch! Watch me!"

David and Rick woke simultaneously. David now stared in shock at his wife, who was now jumping on the spot. Really high.

"Amazing!" Shouted David, "oh Barbara, you can jump!"

"It's a miracle!" Declared Rick.

"Yes, yes it is." Said Barbara. Now, she was actually smiling at him…

Karen Pearson had a busy day today. The presentation was at 9 am sharp. If they were going to get the Colgate contract, then today would be the day.

So, with her alarm going off at 6.30 am, she had plenty of time to make it. She groaned as it chimed, and hit it to snooze. Then, the importance of her day began to bite, and she gradually began to wake up. She checked her phone. Three messages from Kenny. She wasn't going to speak to that cheating bastard this morning. Screw him, she thought.

Karen had lived alone now for three months, since she had found out Kenny had been having an affair with a woman he met at his gym. If she was honest with herself, she couldn't decide whether she should take him back, or see the back of him altogether. She procrastinated. And she hated procrastination in others, which meant that at the moment, Karen hated herself.

After a shower and the careful application of light makeup, she got dressed into her navy blue business suit, pants and skirt first, shirt and jacket next, as per her standard routine. Then she grabbed a protein shake. Kenny's treachery had made her very conscious of her figure, and she was determined to lose fifteen pounds, no matter what.

By now, it was touching 7am. The journey to her office took approximately 30 minutes, but even if it was a bad traffic day, it never took more than 45. That still gave her plenty of time to meet with Bob her boss, and Lianne, her officious but over ambitious assistant. Then, they could do the presentation to Colgate, and the contract, would be theirs. And as a result, that bonus would be all mine, she thought.

She got in her trusty old blue Toyota four-wheel drive, and headed off to the office. The drive was quiet and uneventful, although she did feel a little strange, almost as if she was moving slowly. She hoped she wasn't getting that norovirus that was going round, just before the presentation. That would be just her luck recently, dammit.

She would have to hold the puke in, if that was the case.

She arrived at the office at 7.30 am, to find the underground car park empty. The receptionist didn't start until eight, which was when most of her co-workers started to drift in. Excellent, she thought, she would be able to set up and be ready before Bob and Lianne arrived. They would also have plenty of time for a final rehearsal.

Karen swiped her card in the security lock, and went upstairs to the boardroom where they would conduct the presentations.

She set up the laptop and projector, got herself a coffee, and waited for Bob and Lianne to arrive.

Ten minutes later, the door burst open, first with Patrick, the head of security, followed directly by Bob, then Lianne, and finally by the very harassed looking receptionist, Emily.

"Karen! Patrick said: "What are you doing here?"

"Ummm, I could ask you the same question, Patrick," said Karen. "What's with the S.W.A.T. Team approach? Are you trying to do some kind of security drill? Only, please can you wait until later? We have some Colgate executives coming in for a really important presentation this morning."

"Karen, what are you talking about? said Bob. "The presentation was two days ago. It is Friday today."

Karen looked at Bob, the frowns on her face increasingly creasing that delicate make up as she did so.

"What are you talking about, Bob? Today is Wednesday, and the Colgate executives will be here soon, so you and Lianne and I need to get busy and-"

At this point, Bob cut her off, "today is FRIDAY," he said, speaking slowly now. "You didn't show up. We texted you, called you, but there was nothing. You had just disappeared. Lianne and I ended up doing the presentation together without you. She did I great job, I should add. We got the deal."

Karen said nothing for a few seconds; she tried to process what was going on. Was she dreaming? What was happening?

"Mark has been frantic. He has been everywhere out looking for you after you didn't return home on Wednesday night. Even the Police are involved now."

"Who's Mark?" said Karen.

She saw Bob and Patrick exchange glances at one another, before Bob spoke now in a gentler, more reassuring voice, "why Mark is your fiancé of course."

"I don't know damned Mark, Kenny is my fiancé, at least he was until the bastard cheated on me with that slut from the gym."

"Why don't you take a seat, Miss Pearson, said Patrick. "I think we need to call someone who can help you."

Karen sat down. Perplexed.

Derek had it in his sights now. Finally. He had been stalking the heard for two days, after he first picked up their trial. He just loved to hunt.

The heard hadn't been difficult to track. There was plenty of disturbed ground and scat for him to follow. He had been careful. He wore scent block, and had even camped last night without a fire, just in case the smell of it spooked the herd.

Now he was going to get his reward.

He raised his rifle and aimed at the buck. At that exact moment, the buck raised his head, as if he was trying to scent something. It could be him, Derek was sure of that. He was downwind of the herd. So, what could it be?

Then the heard began to run. Run towards the seeming safety of the forest, across the clearing, which was a good 250 yards across, Derek reckoned. What could be chasing them? Had a mountain lion spooked them or something, he considered.

It was then that he saw it. A black shape. Almost exactly rectangular, spinning deliberately towards the herd. Derek lowered his eyes from the sights to get a better look at it.

It was about 10 feet by ten feet, and it was moving at great speed, whirling and then moving point to point, erratic yet seemingly purposeful at the same time. Now it caught up with the straggler and the last elk just disappeared into it, before its limbs came flying out either side of the mass, while the remaining part of the carcass just dropped below it. Then, it pivoted, dramatically to its right, taking out another elk in exactly the same manner, before the rest vanished into the forest.

The thing hovered for a minute, as if waiting, sensing. Derek ducked his head down, lest it see him. When he raised it a few minutes later, after he had composed himself, he saw that it had vanished. All that remained as evidence of its existence, were the mutilated elk bodies.

"That damn thing killed for fun." Said Derek out loud to the empty forest. It didn't seem the same forest to him now. As, for the first time in his life, he was afraid of what was contained within it...

Randy and Kathy Gates had really had no interest in Bigfoot whatsoever. Randy was a practical man, and had owned the same hardware store for thirty years, which he had inherited off his father, and his father before him. Screws had done him proud, he liked to joke to anyone who would listen. For he had a comfortable life. He and Kathy could travel wherever they wanted. Anywhere in the United States in fact, for they had never wanted to go outside its borders. Not after that weekend in Mexico twenty years ago, which had given them both diarrhea.

Kathy knew Barbara Ellis, but not very well. They both like to play badminton, and they competed in local leagues. It was Kathy that had pointed her out on the local news. He was of course resting on the sofa now, like he always did these days. Life was so very tiring now. When he felt the first pain across his arm, he ignored it. He had things to do, shelves to stock, and he couldn't rely on his assistant Mikey to do that. He had felt some pressure in his chest too, the next day. Again, he had ignored it, and pressed on. Why? Well because that's what men do, he thought. He must not complain. He had not felt the first heart attack at all. The quadruple bypass surgery that followed straight after, had been a complete success, they told him. Except it wasn't. The second and third heart attack soon followed. He had not been up his stairs now in months. He knew the fourth one would finish him. So, here he stayed in this living room come bedroom, waiting for the inevitable.

He did have regrets. He was 60 and obese. He had never exercised and had ignored his type two diabetes and his hypertension for years. Hard work was his motto. That was all his body needed. He and Kathy had lived well. She had never really needed or wanted to work. She had looked after him and the house.

He regretted not having children. He had nobody to leave the hardware store to. Although they had never spoken about it, he knew that Kathy would sell the business as soon as he had passed away. She had no clue about it herself, and he had told her not to trust that idiot Mikey.

Kathy had seen Barbara first on TV. She had been watching the local news in the kitchen making them dinner, while he had been watching the football game in his bedroom come lounge.

"Look at this!" She had run in excitedly, and shown him a grinning Barbara, jumping up and down, next to a big guy called Rick. It was a dumb story about a magical place, where allegedly invisible Bigfoots healed this woman.

"Now why did you just put me through that nonsense?'", said Randy to his wife. "I have just wasted three now valuable remaining minutes of my life."

"I knew you would say that!" Replied Kathy. "I know Barbara Ellis though, and she is a sensible woman. I also know she was dying of cancer. The ladies badminton circle had even discussed creating a memorial for her, but she had turned it down in favor of a donation to cancer research. She was on her way out and desperate I tell you! Now look at her! Randy, she is jumping up and down on live TV!"

"I don't believe a word of it, "said Randy. "If it makes you happy though, I will do it. Call Barbara, get this lunatic Rick's number, and let's get it over with. I will try it."

Two days later, Randy found himself in the circle, after being helped out of the car by Rick and Cathy. The moment Rick started ringing the hand bell, he became a little angry at his own foolishness in agreeing to be here, which he knew would make his heart beat faster. Calm Randy, calm. He said to himself.

He lay down on the cot. And tried to control his breathing. As the others slipped away to sleep, Randy felt like his own life was slipping away. He was angry with himself for indulging his wife with this nonsense. He didn't want to die in this stupid place next to this huge snoring stranger, he had wanted to die holding Kathy's hand. That was what was right, not this.

As he went to sleep, he felt the pain and tightening in his chest first, then he felt a sharp pain in his leg. Then, he felt nothing.

Kathy Ellis woke up at first light. She felt tired and weak, worse than she had ever felt before. Maybe it was just the exhaustion of Randy's illness. She was probably overwhelmed by it all.

She turned to look at Randy, but he wasn't there. He was gone! How could that be! He could barely move on his own!

"Randy! Randy! Where are you?" She called out.

"Behind you!" Declared her husband, and Rick in unison.

"Kathy! Look! I feel great! I can breathe properly again! I am cured! Cured I tell you!"

"Oh, that's wonderful my darling", said Kathy, "but are you sure?"

"Watch this Kathy, Rick suggested I prove it to you by doing what he calls `the Barbara jump` to show you."

"Yes," said Rick, who by now was videoing Randy. "Do it, do it! Do the Barbara jump! Jump! Jump!"

Randy, in his elation, didn't care that Rick was videoing him.

Barbara, also elated, clapped her hands in tandem with the jumps. She should have noticed that her husband was jumping way higher than a sixty year old unfit man could possibly ever manage. Right then though, she didn't care, she was just happy he wasn't dead.

Alex had always loved flowers. She had begun learning their names when she was just three years old in fact. Now, at seven, she possessed an impressive horticultural knowledge. One of the other things she liked best was picnics. Today, Alex and her two brothers Peter and Georgie were off to the flower meadow for a picnic! This was a rare summer treat, as Daddy and Mummy had been working such long hours to keep the business going, that they were normally too exhausted to take them by the weekend. Not today though!

The weather was beautiful, and as the approached the meadow in the car, Alex looked out of its window and saw just how vibrant the colors were. Her tummy hurt a bit. It often did these days. She would forget all about it today though, and just enjoy the meadow. It wouldn't be quite the same though, for she was now on her `special diet`. She couldn't have chocolate cake or peanut butter and jelly sandwiches, for example. So, her parents didn't pack them, as they knew they were two of her favorite things. Her brothers, especially Georgie, had protested, but first to her Daddy, and then to the final court of appeal in her family, Judge Mummy. They had stood their ground though and sorted a compromise in the shape of apple pie and cheese sandwiches. Chocolate milk was a universal foodstuff for the family, which was appreciated by all. So, they were all set.

Mummy and Daddy and her brothers were going to play a little bit of baseball. Before she had been unwell, she had enjoyed playing that, but now she just didn't have the strength anymore.

She was actually happy on her own though. She had brought her little sketchbook with her. On it, she began to sketch all the beautiful little flowers around her. She had brought her coloring pens too, and she used them to really bring out the beautiful violets and vivid blues in the patch right before her. It was then that she heard a little laugh. Almost like a tinkle. She carried on drawing, ignoring it. Suddenly, she heard it again.

Then, she blinked. And then blinked really hard again. They still didn't go away though. For, standing right in front of her, were some little men and women. Three of them looked like fairies from her childhood nursery books, in pretty shimmering dresses. Two had long blonde hair, just like her, and one had red hair. Their hair was all tied up in ponytails. Again, just like her's. With them were two tiny little men. They must be gnomes, she thought. "Hello," said one of the fairies, smiling, as she did so.

"Please allow us to introduce ourselves. My name is Daisy, and this is Charlotte. At this, the other two fairies curtsied.

"And I am Bumble and this is Stiffle," said the gnome with a red hat on. As he did so, he took a bow.

"Why are you here?" said Alex. "Do you live in the flowers?"

"Sort of," said Charlotte. "We were actually going to have a picnic here today, when we heard you playing. Would you like to join our picnic?"

"Oh, I am having one already with Mummy and Daddy and my brothers." Alex replied.
"Ah yes, we know ", said Charlotte. "We have this though!"

As soon as she said it, a piece of chocolate cake magically appeared in her hand on a silver plate.

"Oh, I am sorry little fairy, but I can't eat chocolate cake", said Alex.

"Ah but this one is special", replied the fairy, you can eat this one, and it won't make you sick."

"Really?" Said Charlotte.

"Really," said all the fairies in unison, "we promise."

Ashlen was really pushing it this time. She had always loved running. She had a meeting on Zoom at three with some of the other scientists in her field. She and Tamara were very close to publishing the paper on anthropic selection. She was also fascinated by the idea of parallel universes. They were all the rage in the scientific community at the moment, but she and Tamara now had some novel new angles.

Ashlen began to speed up now, as she saw the edge of the meadow. This was her sprint section. She always sprinted the 800 yards of its width, and the sidewalk that ran at the edge of it, before she touched the tree at the top if it, and then just jogged back to her home.

She pushed harder now, feeling her chest heave, as she headed towards the tree, her vison slightly blurring as she strained her muscles with the effort of this push.

Alex saw it first, even before the fairies did. It was a black rectangular shape, spinning and turning as it headed towards that lady runner. She hadn't seen it. Alex called out: "lady! Lady! Look, wait!"

Now she had. And she turned quickly to run away from it. The thing though, was quicker, and it rushed after straight after her. With one pulse of its opaque shape, she was gone!

"Alex! Alex! You need to be quick now. Please say these words. You must say them three times. 'I want to join the good folk`."

It was Charlotte. All the fairies were looking up at her, frowning and concern all over their faces.

"What?" Said Alex? She was alarmed now, for she could see that the black thing was now moving towards her, rapidly.

Suddenly, Charlotte appeared in front of her, only this time she was full size! And now much taller than Alex. Charlotte grabbed both of Alex's hands as she spoke "You must say, I want to join the Good Folk! You must repeat it three times! Do it now, quick Alex, please! Please trust me!" implored Charlotte.

This time, Alex didn't hesitate: "I want to join the Good Folk! I want to join the Good Folk, I want to join the Good Folk!"

As she said it, both her and Charlotte, instantly shrunk! They were now the size of the other fairies and gnomes. "Quick" said Charlotte. They began to run for the little blue door in the side of the tree. One of the gnomes, who Alex remembered was called Bumble, got their first, and he now beckoned them inside. Except they weren't going to make it. For now, the black thing was upon them, and it was just too far to run. Bluebell and Daisy, who were running on either side of Alex, now grabbed an arm each, and flew in tandem, propelling Alex through the air, toward the door. Stiffle and Charlotte now turned in front of them. Blue fireballs appeared in their hands, which they threw directly at the shape as it charged directly at them. The thing pulsated and then stopped. With that, Alex and the others were through! Charlotte and Stiffle now made for the door. The thing had recovered though, and it continued its pursuit, lunging for the door. Now, first Stiffle, and then Charlotte, were through the door. It was almost too late though, for as she went to close the door the door, the edge of The Black Square touched Charlotte's face. She screamed, falling back into the Fairy World as she did so. Fortunately, Bumble reacted quickly, and slammed the door shut. Then, the door in the little tree vanished, and Alex and the fairies and gnomes, were gone.

Rick lay in bed next to Tammy. He couldn't believe his luck. Was this bullshit actually working? Why were people believing it? Was there something actually to it? Like anyone else, he had not had much luck as a Bigfoot researcher, and attention in him by others had begun to wane. His real job had been slowing down too. For some reason, he just hadn't been able to sell the same amount of cars as he used to. He was just not as sharp as he used to be. This had troubled him. There will be bills to pay, child support obligations to fulfil. So, out of desperation, he had created this notion of magical healing Bigfoots. At first, he liked the attention, then when things had actually started to work and he got some media interest, he worried that he would be found out. Except he hadn't been. He had now taken six people up to *The Circle* to be healed, and they had all returned with powerful testimonies of healing. Those six had also paid his immediate bills. Hell, people were even starting to wear T-shirts with his face on them. He liked that.

What if it wasn't just a con job though and that he was actually on to something? What if he was truly `special`? Six people cured was hard to argue with. He decided he was going to do something that he hadn't done in a very very long time. Since he was a little boy in fact. He was going to pray.

With that, he got to the end of his bed and tried to begin. How though? He had forgotten. Tammy was sound asleep, so he decided he would just whisper it out loud.

"My leader I…" My leader! He laughed to himself. Come on Rick! You can do better than that! Rick cleared his throat!

"My Lord, I ask you for help and guidance, on this special gift you have given me. I thank you for it and ask you what I must do."

With that, a blinding flash filled the room. Rick shielded his eyes at the intensity of it. Then a crackling began, like electricity rumbling. A rumbling sound now permeated the air in his room, almost like a fire. Rick was amazed that Tammy hadn't woken up, but she hadn't. She just lay there. Rick looked aghast now, as a red orb suddenly appeared in the middle of the room. Then it spoke. Its voice was deep, with undulating tones. "Rick, Rick, we have heard you."

"Oh! Said Rick! Tammy! Tammy!"

"She can't hear you," said the voice. "We have made her sleep for now, because we want you to help you, and we want her to not disturb you while we speak to you."

"What do you want?" Said Rick. "We want to help you Rick. We know that you doubted that you were chosen. We are here to tell you that you are."

"We will help you Rick, because we have seen how humanity is suffering. We want to help them heal, Rick. We want to help the children, especially."

"The children?" Said Rick, quizzically.

"Yes the children. They have so much potential you see. We can heal them, and if you bring children to us to be healed, we shall do it. Normal children and their parents can come too. We are love. We want humans to know they can trust us."

"You are chosen, Rick. You are the one."

"I am chosen," repeated Rick." I am the one."

Rick now knew what he had to do…

Sheriff Hawthorne was growing more and more frustrated. Frustrated with the heat, frustrated with the search, frustrated with the dogs. He was proud of that fact, that he was good at what he did. And he had been meticulous. He had brought in search and rescues teams, horse teams for the more mountainous areas, heck even helicopters with thermal cameras. The lot. He hadn't looked forward to it. When he heard a child had gone missing in such bizarre circumstances, and that a woman scientist had gone missing at exactly the same time, he just quickly expected to find a body. Or at least he expected the cadaver dogs to find one. They had found nothing though.

This story that the missing child's parents had come up with, that was just total bullshit! He considered. A killer black square! I mean, come on!

Yet, he had followed every protocol, and the parents wouldn't crack. He had isolated them, interviewed them, been kind to them, threatened them, nothing worked. Yet, here they still were, stubborn as hell, with nothing found. It just didn't make sense. Even the damned kids maintained the story! He looked through the glass at Mrs.Arney. She looked pale. Exhausted but defiant. Some criminals he understood. The ones who stole, the ones who robbed. They always had an excuse why they did it, of course. He had concluded long ago that whatever it boiled down to though, it was always to justify ultimately selfish behavior. These sorts of criminals were a different breed though. Right up there on their own. Child killers. He couldn't help but spit on the floor in disgust. Yes, he was sure they had a special place in hell.

He would never understand them.

Then, he heard a light knock on the door.

Without waiting for an answer, two men immediately burst in.

They were dressed in exactly the same way. Grey suits, black shoes, white shirt, black tie. Average build, average height. It was odd that they were wearing sunglasses indoors, but there was nothing unusual about them apart from that.

"Who are you?" Said Sheriff Hawthorne.

"Allow me to introduce ourselves, said one of the men, smiling. "I am Mr. Saunders. And this is Mr. McGee" .

Jenny Arney's world had transformed in just a few hours. She had been having such a lovely day in the meadow, with her husband and her two children, Peter and Georgie. Then, something she couldn't comprehend had happened. Now, she was here. Her wonderful Alex had gone, swallowed by that THING. That poor woman jogger too! She replayed it back in her mind. Tried to work it all out. Could she have done anything different? She knew in her heart that she would never see Alex again. A mother's intuition, they called it. Well, `they` were right.

"Mrs. Arney.'' A voice broke her from out of her mental replay, back into the real world, and the terrible present before her.

"Mrs. Arney. Two men were now before her. "Yes," she said.

"Allow us to introduce ourselves, my name is Mr. Saunders, and this is Mr. McGee."

"What do you want," she said, are you here to ask me my story again. I have told it to the Sheriff and different police officers at least twenty times now. I suppose you want to hear it again too." She sighed at this last comment.

"Not at all, Mrs. Arney," said Mr. Saunders. "In fact, we are here to help you."

"Help me?" She said. "How can you help me? All I want is help finding Alex."

Mr. Saunders reached over and grabbed both her hands, with his. For some reason, Jenny found herself unable to withdraw as he did so, even though his hands felt icy cold.

"We can help you Mrs. Arney."

"Hhhhow?" Jenny shivered at his touch.

"Well, I am afraid to say that your lovely little daughter can't be found. That jogger can't be found either. Such a brilliant mind. Such a shame. Such terrible tragedies."

"Can't you help? Can't you find that thing? That thing that did this?"

"Ah, we can certainly help with that! You didn't see a `thing `Mrs. Arney. You saw a person."

"What I saw, Mr. Saunders was a huge black square swallow a helpless woman. That same damn thing undoubtedly took my poor daughter!"

"Ah but you didn't though? You and I both know that nobody is going to believe that story," said Mr. Saunders.

"You know who is the prime suspect in cases like this, Mrs.Arney? The husband. Then any other male relations, or boyfriends. If you persist with this story, social services will undoubtedly take Peter and Georgie into care. You don't want that for them do you? Mr. McGee and I have spoken to them, and they seem such nice boys."

At this Mr. Saunders stopped and looked at her, smiling as he did so.

Mrs. Arney returned his smile with a hard stare "No, Mr. Saunders, I don't want that."

"Excellent!" Said Mr. Saunders. That is how we can help you then! At this' he lifted his finger in delight. He then went on: "we can provide you with a plausible suspect. We can stop your children from being taken away. All you need to do, is speak to Mr. Arney, and make sure he is on board. Of course, if he isn't- ''

"He will be", said Jenny, finally finding the strength to withdraw her hands from Mr. Saunders clutches as she did so ." My husband and children will agree with me."

"Well then," said Mr. Saunders, turning now to his colleague as he did so, "I think we have a deal Mr. McGee. Mr. McGee just nodded and smiled. If Jenny had not been in such distress, she would have noticed that Mr. McGee's smile was just a little off. That there was something unnatural about it.


John and Sally Lomax had really enjoyed their last few years on the road. When he had retired from the automobile factory, they had gone full at it to pursue their dream. They had bought a lovely new motor home. They had sold off most of what they had. John had regarded them as little more than useless trinkets, but Sally had sniffled a bit at some of the items they had sold off. Misplaced sentimentality,

John had thought. You don't really need possessions. They had then set out on the road. First, they had travelled all the way up to Alaska. John had always wanted to see it, but it had always been an expensive place to reach. He hadn't been disappointed. Its beauty was just breathtaking.

 They had bought a beagle puppy, Sally had named her Jess, and the three of them had pursued adventure across the United States together. They had headed first to Louisiana, as Sally had always loved Cajun food, and she wanted to try it in an authentic setting. Then Gettysburg, as John had always been fascinated by the history of the Civil War. Since then, they had been all over the place. Everywhere you could think of. It had been amazing. They had had a fabulous time. Now John was worried though. And his worry had led him to this trailer park in the middle of nowheresville, Oregon. He hadn't told Sally yet, but he knew that the money was already starting to run out. John wasn't a complete idiot, he told himself. He had known for example, that their little home would always depreciate in value no matter what. He had even budgeted for it. With their savings and pensions carefully managed, they could easily have afforded a new one right about this time .Except that John had never been that good at managing his money, and well, Sally was useless at it.

 Then the pain in his back started. He had slipped disc years ago, as a younger man. Now, it seared through him, a vein of pure pain. He had had anti –inflammatory pills at first to help him with it. They weren't really working though. They couldn't really afford a Doctor, let alone an operation. John knew this. So, for the first time in five years, John actually found himself worried for the future. He had parked their motor home here, on the edge of these woods, to have a think, to plan a strategy. One thing was for certain. He and Sally would need to talk.

The first time he heard it was a few days ago. He had sat outside, smoking a cigarette. Sally hated him smoking. He didn't really like it himself, if truth be known. He limited himself to just two or three a day now. Mainly in the evening, with his medicinal whisky before bed.

The first night, he had heard just a growling noise. He had thought it was a dog at first. Then, by the time he had got to his second cigarette, he realized it was something... else. He had felt fear. A coldness in his body. They were on the end of the camping area, the spot closest to the woods, and for the first time in a long time, John felt vulnerable.

The next day he had got the old revolver out, and loaded it. When Sally had asked him why, he had merely shrugged and said you couldn't be too careful in case of prowlers. That had satisfied her, for that day anyway. The second night, there was no doubt though. They were both asleep when it came. Round about 3am. It had banged on the sides of their little home and, wait! It even seemed like it was laughing! Sally had woken up at this "What is it, John?" She said "a man or what?"

John felt it was more likely a `what` than a man`, but of course he didn't share that with Sally.

The following morning, Sally had wanted to leave right away, but John had persuaded her it must be their imaginations. After an hour or so, he talked her round to believing it was just a coyote, and that they had both misinterpreted it. He didn't tell her the real reason why. That was that he had done a special deal with the owner of the RV Park. At first, he had refused to allow them to stay. However, John had sweetened the deal by offering that he would pay for a two week stay. This, the owner had reluctantly agreed to, but only on condition that they parked here, on the edge of the Park. If they left now, they would lose all that money. It had been made very clear to him that there would be no refunds. So, they had to stick it out, at least for one more night. If it came again tonight, John told himself, then that would be it.

That night, John sat outside the camper van. It was 11 pm, and he was on his fourth whisky. With each one, he had had a cigarette, so now he was on twice his normal dosage of both. Sally had gone to bed an hour ago. All was really quiet. Then, he heard a movement, just slight, just to the side of him. He turned, and instinctively grabbed the gun as he did so. "Jess, Jess, go see!" He said to his little beagle, who by now had got up, and was barking furiously at something on the other side of their mobile home. Jess needed no further instruction, as she bolted off in that direction. Emboldened by his dogs actions, John hurried straight after her. In fact, he was probably only ten paces behind her, which was enough distance to give the creature time to rip his beloved pet in two, and fling the pieces back at him. John staggered back, at the impact.

Before him, stood a giant creature, which looked like a wolf, only it was upright. It had a huge snout, from which protruded a seemingly impossible number of teeth in all directions. Some jutting to the side, some up, some down. It eyes glowed red, and John could feel its malice. He fired, straight into its shoulder. The creature didn't move, even at the impact. The bullet just seemed to be absorbed within it, John thought. Then it laughed, laughed as it soaked up his fear. John raised his gun to fire again; it was all he could do really. He never had time to see the claws the creature possessed, but he was able to feel them as they ripped through his torso. The creature penetrated straight through John's body, and gripped his intestines, as it raised his agonized face to its own, staring into the humans eyes, seemingly savoring the intensity of the suffering it was observing. Then it dropped John, in direct response to Sally's screams, which were coming from the steps of the mobile home. On its approach, she ran inside, shutting the door as it did so. At this, the creature gave another of its throaty laughs, before it ripped the door clean off, with one effortless lunge.

Now it stood in front of her salivating. She cowered in terror as it waited. Sniffing the air, savoring the taste of her fear.

Then, as she tried to let out a scream, it leapt at her. At first, Sally was quick, quicker even than it expected, and as she ducked its first slash missed, tearing the delicate fabric of the curtains behind her. Sally now rushed for the open door, screaming as she did so. She made it to the step, but that was as far as she got before it dragged her by her hair back into the mobile home, and to her death.

When Ernie Thomas had heard the screams, he had come out immediately. A Vietnam vet, he was nobody's fool and as bold as thunder. He had his shotgun ready, and although horrified at the creature before him, he did have the composure to fire it straight into the torso of whatever monster he had just seen before him. The creature absorbed the wound, but this time it clutched at it. It looked at Ernie angrily, and for an instant he thought he was dead, for it surely could have leapt at him. It didn't though. At first, it stood there, and sniffed the air. Then it snorted, and instead of attacking, it turned to the right of the van, and began running straight into the woods.

Ernie fired straight after it: "you bastard!" He shouted, "don't ever come back."

Detective Parker was there early to meet his two guests. Also in attendance was a female officer, who stood with Ernie Thomas who they had also requested to speak to.

"We would just dismiss the witness as mistaken, or his account as some drunken ramblings. Were it not of course for the vicious murders, and these slash marks. "He held the torn fabric up, to them as he spoke.

"What sort of weapon does this? We are baffled."

Neither men replied to this comments, so the Detective just shrugged and led them over to where Ernie Thomas stood.

"Mr. Thomas, he said, "allow me to introduce you to Mr. Saunders and Mr. McGee. They would like to talk to you about what you saw."

"It was the darndest thing! Said Ernie, not waiting for any questions. "It looked like some sort of damn werewolf! I shot it and it ran into the woods. You can call me a crazy old man if you want to, but that's what I saw!"

"What did it do immediately after you shot it?" Asked Mr. Saunders.

This question made Ernie hesitate and he narrowed his eyes at Mr. Saunders as he replied, "well it seemed to sniff at something in the air, I don't know what. Then it ran off."

"Thank you, Mr. Thomas, said Saunders. "There will be no further questions."

"That's it?" Said detective Parker.

"That's it," said Mr. Saunders, "Mr. McGee thank you all for your time. Good luck with the rest of your investigation."

When he was safely out of hearing of them all, he turned to Mr. McGee and said "why Mr. McGee, I do believe they are becoming bolder. This is a very serious matter."

"Very serious indeed, "said Mr. McGee, by way of agreement.

Melissa Kennedy was top of her class in mathematics and science. She wanted to be a scientist. She was tall for her year as well. She was nine years old, but looked twelve. She had enjoyed a lot of boys games, and this one, climbing trees, was truly one of her favorites. Her favorite was a big oak in the park. Her Mum, and Mark's Mum liked to walk their dogs together in the park, so she had plenty of time to climb trees with Noah.

She ran straight over. It was a little more difficult than it used to be, as she had been feeling really breathless recently. She would manage though. Noah ran to his favorite tree, another Oak, similar to hers. They liked to climb to the middle branches, and shout at one another from there. In their game, they were the secret tribe of tree people. At least for the twenty minutes it took their Mum's to traverse the circular route around the park.

"It's risky," said Bumble. "We have to try," said Charlotte. "She is big, too old," said Bluebell." "Ah yes, said Stiffle,"but *he* commanded it." He said we must beat the others to it. "

"Then we must obey," said Daisy. "I will try first."

"So be it." Said Bumble.

As Melissa approached the tree, she heard some tiny voices. They were musical and lyrical, like little silver bells.

"Melissa! Melissa!" Won't you come and play with us? Won't you come and play please .We want you to come and sing."

Melissa had now got to the base of the tree. And she stood their panting, as physical effort was getting harder for her now than it used to be, although she didn't know why.

Below her, were what looked like five tiny people? Three females and two males. And they were dancing. The females were spinning in a circle, and sunlight was literally glistening off their wings as they spun. The two males, were dancing a sort of jig.

"Who are you," said Melissa?

At this, the fairies stopped dancing, and all of the little people clapped their hands. Now, one of the blonde ones spoke "excellent, you can see us! " My name is Daisy, and my little friends here are Bluebell, and Charlotte." After their introduction, the fairies all curtsied in unison. Melissa thought them all very pretty indeed.

"And I am Bumble, and this is Stiffle," said the gnome with the red hat. They both then took a bow.

"We would like you to play with us. And look, we have chocolate dipped strawberries, your favorite, "said Charlotte.

Melissa frowned "I am not going anywhere, with you, and I am not eating anything you give me, little fairy! You are just a figment of my imagination."

*The Black Square* was making its way across the park now, spinning and twirling towards the child, its inevitable target.

Charlotte now spoke more urgently "Melissa, Melissa! You must be quick, eat a strawberry please, just one! Quick, before that thing behind you gets here! "

"Aha! Said Melissa ''my imagination is particularly fertile today! You want me to look around! Well, I am not going to, I tell you!"

Melissa now folded her arms, and stared down the fairies defiantly.

"I will see if I can give you just a minute longer, "said Bluebell, who now stepped in front of Melissa, and began throwing blue fireballs into *The Black Square*. Each one slowed it a little, almost like it was stopping to collect them, but it still move inexorably forward.

"Melissa, just indulge me for a second, please," said Charlotte. "Your rational mind tells you that we don't exist. I understand that.

However, aside from that, what if there is a real threat actually behind you and you now choose to ignore it? What will your stubbornness do for science or the danger you are exposing yourself to, answer me that?"

Melissa considered what Charlotte had had to say, and then turned, just as *The Black Square* was almost upon them. Her eyes widened "Help me! Help me". She said to Charlotte!

"Take a strawberry quick!" Said Charlotte.

By now, Bumble, Stiffle and Daisy were all throwing fireballs at *The Black Square*. Even as she took a strawberry though, it was upon Melissa and it sucked her in, taking a hapless Bluebell with her, who turned and dived just too late, as it twisted to lunge for its prey.

Stiffle and Bumble had made it to the door now, and Daisy was right behind them. Now it moved to envelope Charlotte, who was last towards the door, as she had toppled over when Melissa had been absorbed. Instead of taking her though, it hesitated, before again lunging forward. This hesitation was enough though, to allow Charlotte to get through the door. Bumble slammed it shut immediately. With that, it disappeared.

## Chapter Four

### The Healing

This was the biggest crowd that Rick had ever brought to `The Circle`, as he liked to call it. He had now given it a name. There was something of a convoy. Two sick kids and one parent for each of them, driven by Mike, while he and Ian and Rick's son Tim, had also joined them. Not only was this unusual, but this time they also had a reporter with them, a woman named Kim Souzal, from the local TV news, and her camera man.

They had wanted to drive their own truck of course, but he had refused that. The only stipulation he made of them was that they had to come with him, and that they must never reveal the location. Although the route was difficult as it weaved and twisted its way up the mountain, he knew it would not be impossible to find `The Circle`.

He was growing in confidence now. Ever since they had spoken to him, he had got stronger. They had told him to do this.

His beloved wife Jennifer had made some t-shorts for the kids with his face on. Mike and Rick also sported them. He liked that he liked to feel special. Like he was chosen. Which he now was. As he had told Ms. Souzal when she first interviewed him, this tribe of forest people was good. And they wouldn't hurt anyone. They could heal. He had seen her cameraman, Doug, smirking. Well, pretty soon he would show him. He hadn't told Kim Souzal yet that they were from another world. He would wait until after the healing.

Rick went through the rituals like normal. First the hand bell. Then the offerings of food. He let the children put out the donuts in the bowl this time, and he joked of course that he had plenty for everyone in the morning. Both the children had terminal cancer. It was easy to read the nervous desperation in their parent's eyes. It was also easy to read the distrust and suspicion in the mannerisms of Ms. Souzal and her cameraman. Of course, for this trip he wasn't charging. Mike had unofficially sponsored this trip, but that was their secret. He couldn't work for nothing, he considered. After all, he had bills to pay like anybody else.

The cots were all carefully laid out now. Rick was worried that not everyone would be able to sleep. Ever since Ian had built the machine though, they had had no problem with that, so why should they tonight? Ms. Souzal had wanted to film everything, but they had told him not to let her film Ian's machine, so he wouldn't let her do that. Instead, he had Ian pull it from the trunk and switch it on surreptitiously, while Mike played the guitar and he and the children sang together. It was a good visual, he knew that, and Ms. Souzal and the cameraman were completely absorbed in it. Nobody missed the nondescript Ian for a few minutes.

Eventually, it was time for bed. Rick thought that of all of them he would find it hardest to sleep. He didn't though, and soon he found himself drifting off.

He awoke the next morning to the sounds of children's laughter.

Amazingly, he was the last one to wake up. Everyone else was already up and about, running and cheering.

It was Ms. Souzal and a now grinning Doug the cameraman who approached him first.

"Hey sleepy head!" She said. "We tried to wake you, but you wouldn't stir at first. It's good to see you up now. Have you seen the children? Lorenzo there could barely even walk yesterday, as you know. Look at him now! I can't say I understand how all this works, and I know we have to do medical tests when we get back as agreed, but I am amazed! Lorenzo! Lorenzo! Hey Misty! You two kids! Show Rick what you can do! Do the` Barbara jump`."

And they did. Both children leapt inordinately high into the air, as the adults encouraged them to jump. Their parents beamed with joy. As did Mike and Rick. As did Ms. Souzal and her cameraman.

None of them noticed the two figures stood by the little door, in the tree. One was a beautiful tiny winged fairy, with red hair, and just the smallest scar on her face. The other a little gnome with a red hat, who was frowning.

Charlotte and Bumble watched the laughter with growing concern. They couldn't stay long in that place. For the atmosphere here was toxic to them. It felt heavy and oppressive.

"We have to tell him." Said Bumble.

"Without a doubt". Said Charlotte.

With that, Bumble shut the door, and they and it, disappeared....

Jamie had been pretty nervous about going to meet Penny's parents. They had been dating six months though, and he had fallen in love. He knew that this was a logical next step, and he couldn't refuse. He had dodged two dinners so far. He would feel uncomfortable. Her Dad was a former Marine, a tough guy, and Jamie thought he might struggle under his inscrutable gaze. However, when Jenny suggested a hike in the woods, he felt couldn't refuse. And he had to say, it had gone pretty well so far. Ted, Penny's Dad, had been fine so far, pleasant and jolly, and her Mum Pam, who Penny resembled, was really sweet. Just like his Penny. Ah, there, he had said it to himself. His Penny. There would come a time when he would have to speak to her Dad about an engagement, as things were going so well. Not just yet though. She could wait a little bit longer, say three months. That would seem an appropriate length of time.

Penny was holding his hand now and smiling. She looked so happy. They were slightly behind her parents now, as the trail narrowed through the woods. Respectfully, they let Penny's Dad lead the way, as he limped from his injury, and he was a proud man. Suddenly though, he and Penny's Mum halted. Halted so abruptly, that Jamie and Penny nearly slammed into the back of them, as they were busy looking at each other, rather than the trail in front of them.

"Well, I'll be damned." Said Ted.

Straight in front of them, right in the middle of the trail in fact, was a mahogany staircase. It was beautifully carved, thought Jamie. It looked antique. The staircase had about twenty steps leading up it, and then most curiously it just disappeared into nothing!

"Isn't it the strangest thing you have ever seen?" Said Pam.

"Let's go up it, Jamie, "Said Penny. "What's the point? Said Jamie "It doesn't go anywhere."

"Just to get a photo," she replied. "c'mon let's go." At this she grabbed his hand.

"Dad, will you take a picture of me and Jamie at the top, please?"

"Sure, "replied Ted. He stood there, poised with his daughter's cell phone ready. Jamie and Penny meanwhile chuckled to each other as they went up the stairs and turned to waive when they reached the top. That was the last thing they did though, for as they turned to face Ted, there was a tearing sound, and whoosh, and then they were gone!

At first, Ted and Pam laughed, thinking it was some kind of magic trick connected with the staircase. Then, they began to realize it wasn't.

"Penny, please come down now, implored Pam. Your Dad and I have had enough of the game now."

"I am going to have to go up there myself, said Ted. "We need to find out what's going on."

He climbed the staircase. As he got to the top, he could see a red mist, which wasn't visible from the ground below.

"There's something here!" He shouted down to his wife below.

"Be very careful," she replied. Ted entered the mist. In the second that he did so, he found himself falling. He landed with a crunch, which happened simultaneously with his wife's scream. Ted had broken his ankle. And as he looked around through gritted teeth, he could see that both the staircase and his beloved daughter had both completely vanished…

"You guys are not seriously going to visit this loon, are you?" Said Philip, between mouthfuls of beer. The three friends had arranged to meet for Friday night drinks, in their local bar, as they nearly always did.

"I mean, all this healing business with kids, it has got to be nonsense."

"I think it probably is, says Jake. "And really, I am not too interested in that. I am interested in the idea that Rick has become something of a cultural phenomenon though. He is gathering quite the celebrity status now. However, what I am really interested in is the fact that he has alleged Bigfoots in the area. Many of the people who attend `The Circle`, report seeing Bigfoots and hearing them. Rick has recorded some interesting vocals with his parabolic microphone.

"The people who go to his place are all crazy asses!" Philip exclaimed, "Have you seen those damn t-shirts they are wearing."

"Yes, of course, "replied Jake. "The way I see it though, I am after clear, very clear DNA evidence of a possible Bigfoot. Rick has posted numerous photos of the bowls he uses to leave out what he calls `offerings` for the creatures. If I can get some hair off those bowls, then I can give something tangible to Professor Lockwood to test."

"Yes, and I will be coming with him too, "said Simon. So I will help to keep the crazy down to a minimum."

"You will still be outnumbered though, "said Philip. "I don't think that crazy ass goes anywhere without his two sidekicks, Mike and Ian. Like creepy henchmen. Have you seen them on TV? All they ever seem to do is smile."

"That's true," said Jake. "The way I see it though is that we have nothing to lose. Me and Simon are not going to get sucked in by Rick's bullshit. And we have just a chance, just a faint chance, of getting the DNA evidence we need. After that, we can move on with the rest of our research. We will rendezvous with you in Seattle five days after we finish up in Oregon."

"Okay, be safe boys, is all I am saying," Philip replied.

"Well, so far we are getting on fine with Rick, both of us had to submit to a two hour telephone `interview` before he would even let us go".

"It sounds to me like he was assessing whether you could be manipulated easily," said Philip. "Were any of the questions strange, or odd, in any way to either of you?"

"Not really," said Simon, shrugging as he did so. "He just asked about what my preferences were. Like food and colors. Stuff like that. He did ask if I was in a relationship, but when I said yes, he didn't probe any further."

"I had exactly the same sort of questions," said Jake. "Except there was one thing right at the end." He said `they` were looking forward to seeing me."

"Who the hell are they?" Said Philip.

"I asked the same question, and he said it was the Bigfoots."

"Well, he never said that to me, so they obviously don't give a shit about seeing me," joked Simon.

"There you go then! Said Philip "Crazy as a moonbeam!" The Bigfoots are looking forward to meeting you! I will be very glad to see you safe in Seattle, I can tell you."

"Until then, "said Jake. With that, they clinked each other's beer glasses together, before leaving the bar.

Two days later, Jake and Mike, flew into Seattle and picked up their hire car. From there, they were to make the short journey over to Rick's house, where they would spend the night as guest of him and his wife Jennifer, before making the seven hour drive to down to `The Circle` in Oregon, the next day.

The night before the flight, Jake had been restless; he had even had a nightmare, which had awoken him.

Now though, with the investigation underway, he was focused. Something told him that he would need all his energy over the next few days.

# CHAPTER FIVE

## THE BATTLE OF THE CIRCLE

Jake and Simon's drive to Rick's House in Bellingham was uneventful. And they arrived there, courtesy of the GPS, by 5pm. Still with plenty of time for dinner. Rick and his wife Jennifer were attentive hosts, serving big stakes with pineapple for dinner. Rick explained that he had already arranged supplies with Mike and Ian, who would meet them at 5.30am outside Rick's house, ready for the seven hour drive down. The dinner was delicious, Jake thought, and he didn't have to say very much, which also suited him, as Rick did more than enough talking for the four people around the table. Most of what Rick had to say was a reiteration of the odd protocols that he had insisted on during his telephone conversations with him and Simon. There were to be no campfires during their stay, and no alcohol. Rick explained that the Bigfoots would be scared to approach by the fire. "My studies have led me to conclude that they are nocturnal creatures, pushed into the darkness by the avarice of man." Rick spoke with an absolute certainty about all of his assertions, and as he carried on, and Jake got the impression that they were not to be challenged. For to do so might mean, even at this late stage, that Rick's offer to take them with him might be rescinded.

Rick had already asked if they smoked. Rick said he disapproved, but he understood that Jake and Simon did want to smoke the occasional cigar, and so they were permitted to smoke precisely at the four o'clock position on the dial. Rick explained he would give a tour when they first got there, and explain it all to them. They were free to wander anywhere during the day. Except one place. "I will show you the hillside where the caves are .That is where they sleep during the day. You must not under any circumstances go there. Are we agreed?" Said Rick.

"Yes," said Jake and Simon. Jake reckoned that it was probably the first time they had both been `allowed` to speak in at least twenty minutes.

The one thing that Rick was most keen to emphasize was the importance of sleep. "It can be difficult I know, to really sleep. When you are excited. Especially, if you have an encounter with the Bigfoots. I am sure you will though Jake. In fact, I am certain that you will."

At this point, Rick turned to his wife Jennifer, and nodded. She had barely spoken three or four words since the arrived. She had however, maintained the same incredulous smile on her face. Now, she produced a little recorder from her handbag by her feet. Again, without saying anything, she pressed the button. Rick, of course provided the context to what they were saying. "As you know, I spend four days at `The Circle` every month. I am lucky to be able to do this because my lovely wife encourages it and supports it through her hard work as a Dentist." With this, he looked at Jennifer, who returned his smile with another inane one of her own.

Rick motioned Jennifer to push the play button with a nod of his head, which he duly did.

At first, there was nothing but static, then a crackling...then very clearly and beyond a shadow of a doubt, he heard what sounded like a female whispering "Jake ....Jake ... Jake..."

Ever the showman even in his own house, this was the moment he had been waiting for. Even he didn't speak for a few seconds, for he was savoring the moment, enjoying the obvious surprise on Jake's and Simon's faces.

"Mike, Ian and I all had such a laugh when we saw this, "said Rick. " Just so you are perfectly clear, that gentlemen, was a female Bigfoot. She has told me she is called Qwallee."

"Told you?" Said Jake, "I thought you were all sleeping when the Bigfoots came in. "

"Yes we are, but sometimes they speak to me in my dreams."

"How do they do that?" Said Jake, looking at Simon as he did so." All in good time, my friend, all in good time. You will see." In the meantime, though, Ian Mike and I did have a laugh at that message for you. You clearly have an admirer.

"Well thank you ", said Jake, "but I like my women without hairy backs."

They all laughed at this, even Jennifer, who seemed to rock her head back quite far as she was doing it Jake noticed, almost like she was learning how to do it.

"Now there just remains one thing, gentlemen," said Rick. The non -disclosure agreement. As we discussed on the phone, I want you to sign this to say that you will never reveal the location of `The Circle`, without my consent."

Simon looked at Jake. They had had a lengthy conversation about this non-disclosure agreement before they came out to meet Rick. Jake hadn't established the exact location of the place, other than it was somewhere near Bend in Oregon. He had established however that it was on public land, in the hills surrounding it. As such, Jake knew that the non-disclosure agreement had no validity whatsoever.

"If it makes him happy, and it does no harm, then I am happy to just go with it," Jake had explained to Simon, the week before.

"No worries," Simon had said "but this guy seems to need a lot of ego stroking. I hope it is all worth it, and we get the samples we need."

"So do I,"Jake had replied. "It's going to be a long shot, but we will see."

That night, Jake had a restless sleep. He didn't know why, but he just could not relax. His heart seemed to be racing. Almost like he was experiencing hyper vigilance before he had even got to, `The Circle`.

He was glad of the morning. As was Simon, who emerged from his room looking a little rough, Jake thought.

'Bad night's sleep?" Said Jake.

"Yes, "replied Simon. "Let's do this thing."

They said goodbye to Jennifer, who was immaculate even that early in the morning, and headed towards Rick's truck.

Rick wanted to get breakfast on the road, so they just waved at Ian and Mike in their parked truck before they all set off.

In the couple of hours before breakfast, even Rick was quiet and self-absorbed, so it gave Jake and Mike an opportunity to snooze.

After proper introductions in the diner, Rick then amused himself, by showing Mike and Ian the pictures he had taken of Jake and Simon while sleeping. By this stage, Jake felt he needed a break from Rick, so he deliberately sat himself opposite Mike, the smaller of the two guys. Jake was hungry, but he noticed that Rick, Ian and Mike ordered gargantuan breakfasts. Eggs, bacon, pancakes sausage, hash browns, the lot. Mike was small and skinny Jake observed, yet even he had polished off his entire breakfast before either he or Simon were even a third of the way through theirs.

As he was going to be with them for the next few days, Jake decided he would try hard to build a relationship with them as best he could and try to penetrate the grins that they both had on their faces. The same grin that Jennifer had had. Which he now began to find a little disturbing.

"So, are you guys excited about going back to `The Circle`, again?"

Said Jake.

"For me now," said Mike it is more a sense of enlightenment. "The Bigfoots give me comfort now, comfort in a way I never thought possible."

"How do they give you comfort, Mike?" Sid Jake.

"Well, they are really wonderful in what they do. They just seem to care for you and nurture you. It is like a feeling inside you. I can't really explain."

"That's right," said Ian. I will confess to you Jake, that before I went to `The Circle`, I was terribly lonely. I had not had any sort of relationship with a woman in over ten years. Now I have my Amy. I am delighted. It is the best move I have ever made. Amy loves me."

"And you think this is because of the Bigfoots?" Said Jake .Although he tried to disguise it a little in his voice, he realized it sounded incredulous.

"Yes indeed" said Ian. "I know it sounds implausible, and I understand right now, that you might be skeptical. I have been a carpenter all my life and I like to consider myself both a practical and honorable man. You are blessed though, it is now an opportunity to see it and experience it for yourself."

"Yes," said Mike , "Rick doesn't just take anyone up here, he carefully selects those he does take. You have been chosen."

"Well, I guess that's a compliment," said Jake.

"More than a compliment, it's an honor," replied Ian.

Outside the diner, Jake grabbed Simon, for a cigarette. As the others didn't smoke, it was an opportunity to be alone with his friend.

"These guys really think there is something special going on here, that these magical healing Bigfoots are real," said Jake.

"You are telling me,"said Simon. "It was quite clear to me over breakfast that Rick thinks of himself as some sort of prophet."

"I think the others think that too, "said Jake. "I have a feeling that it's going to be a long few days."

"I have no doubt about that," said Simon. "I wish we had brought the hire car with us."

"Well," he said the paths up there were very bad, covered in branches and we would get its paintwork scratched," replied Jake.

"I hope they were serious, and we are not some kind of sacrifice or something," joked Simon.

"Yes! Ha ha! I think we just have to endure the next few days, and hope that we get some hair samples to be analyzed."

The rest of the journey down was uneventful, though Jake and Simon were glad of the coffees in town by the time they go there.

"This last part of the journey will be just about thirty minutes," said Rick, then we will be there."

"Good stuff," said Simon," "I am really getting stiff."

The tracks leading up to `*The Circle*`, were exactly as Rick had described. After leaving the last of the houses in the valley below, they twisted and turned up the mountainside, for miles and miles. In many places they had to completely stop and pull branches from the road or endure a screeching sound as they hit the side doors of the trucks.

"I am now really glad I didn't bring the hire car," said Simon.

Eventually, the two trucks pulled into `The Circle`, and Rick then said "please follow me gentlemen, and do exactly as I ask from now on. As long as we are here. Okay?"

"Okay," said Jake and Simon, in tandem.

Rick then got out of the car, and Rick put them carefully into a line. He was at the center of it, with Jake to the left of him and Ian to the right. Simon and Mike took the ends. Then, after ringing the bell, he began to speak:

"People of the forest, our guardian souls, I, as your chosen ambassador, ask you to welcome Jake and Simon, as our guests, during their stay here."

Then he turned to Jake and Simon, "now you speak to them," he said.

Jake and Simon looked at one another for a second, before Jake said "err, yes, we are glad to be here, and we look forward to seeing you."

"We come in peace," said Simon, in a thin watery voice.

Rick seemed satisfied with this, so they were then all able to begin unpacking.

The cots were all laid out in a neat row, by Jake Simon and Rick. Mike bean setting up the tables, putting water, a cooking stove and some food on it for tonight's meal, which he had volunteered to cook.

Rick then asked Jake and Simon to come over to the table. "I have something important to show you, "he said.

"These are the gifting bowls," said Rick, "and we like to record what has been taken each day. We will photograph them before we put them out, and then inspect them in the morning."

With that, he carefully placed three Cheetos in each bowl, and three donuts.

"I would like to smear a little jam around the bowls, if you don't mind Rick, said Jake. I know you don't want me to use hair traps or trail cams, but a bit of jam might accidentally catch some hairs, which is what I am after."

"Agreed, "said Rick. With this, Jake donned some latex gloves, and smeared the jam around the sides. By now, it was starting to get dark, and they walked into the forest, to leave out the gifting bowls.

"Why don't you just leave them in the camp for the Bigfoots to eat, or just outside it? "Asked Jake.

"We have tried that,"said Rick, "but they won't take it . Only when we put it slightly away from the camp do they take it."

"I have another question though," said Jake, who knew he was pushing it a bit, but felt he had to ask. " How do you know that the Bigfoots are actually the one's taking the food, if you don't actually see them?"

Rick looked a little affronted by the question, as Jake imagined he might be, but he thought it important to ask anyway. "They told me it was THEM who take the food, and their word is more than enough for me. As it will be for you too Jake, as you will see."

By the time they returned, Mike had cooked the turkey burgers, which he handed to them on a paper plate, with a bun.

Over dinner, Rick explained how `The Circle` 'worked.

"The first night is normally quiet, not much happens. It takes until the second night for them to get going .And we are normally pretty tired anyway from the long drive down. So normally, we just go to sleep after and relax on the first night. It is the second night when thing's normally really begin, and activity starts to happen." Tomorrow night will be fun. However, I want you to always remain in `The Circle` after dark, I have promised them that. I also want to stick to our familiar routine, so they can trust us and relax. Tomorrow night, we will play music and relax. Mike, Ian and I will point out activity should it happen in the circle, treating it as a 24 hour clock dial. So, if we say `three o'clock, ` you can go over there, only don't step into the forest. Okay?"

"Yes, we understand," said Jake.

"Excellent!" Said Rick, "with that, I will bid you goodnight then gentlemen."

They all quickly retired to their cots after that. Jake thought he would have great difficulty going to sleep, and at first, he just listened out for sounds in the forest. Then though, he too drifted into the deepest sleep….

The next morning, Jake awoke and was immediately alert. He could feel his heart racing, thumping in his chest. He sat up and looked around. Mike and Ian were chatting by the camping tables, with Mike making breakfast. Rick was nowhere to be seen. While Simon was still sleeping on his cot, with his blanket wrapped tightly around him.

Now Jake had to suck in and breathe hard just to even sit up, such was the unsettling feeling he was having. What was wrong with him? He only smoked a couple of cigarettes a day, he worked out as well. Why was he feeling so bad? He sat up and felt a little better, although he still felt dizzy.

"Good Morning, said Rick" Mike has heated some pancakes. "After you two sleepy heads have had some breakfast, we can go and collect the gifting bowls."

"Okay great," said Jake, who by now was waking Simon up.

"How did you sleep?" "Like a log," said Simon. "Really deep. Which is strange for the outdoors, as normally I sleep light. How about you?"

"Oh, I feel a bit rough today," said Jake. "Like I am anxious for some reason. Other than that, I am fine."

The two gratefully consumed the pancakes offered to them by a smiling Mike. Then it was off to the gifting bowls.

"Ah you can see," said Rick, look fingerprints. Clearly visible on each of the bowls were huge prints, much bigger than that of a man.

Jake and Simon immediately photographed them. Dermal ridges were not visible, as they were smudged, but food had been taken from both bowls. Both a donut and a cheeto from each, in fact.

"As I said, they don't like to each much on the first night, and there isn't much activity usually. Just like last night. Tonight is when the party really begins!" Said Rick.

By now, they were back at camp, and Rick briefly discussed the food missing from the bowls with Mike and Ian.

After that, they packed up the breakfast things while Rick outlined the plans for the day "We are going to get some supplies and do a few errands in town. You guys are welcome to stay here if you like. And explore. You are free to go anywhere you want to, except the caves where they live. Do you promise you won't do that?" Said Rick.

"Yes, we both promise," said Jake and Simon consecutively.

After Rick had left, Jake and Simon began getting their gear together 'Well, I think it's important that we trek just about everywhere we can here, to really get a feel of the whole area," said Jake.

"I agree," said Simon. We can also skirt the edges of the perimeter of `The Circle`, and see what the brush is like, and how easily it is for things to move around."

First, they headed off through the path at the twelve o'clock position into the woods. The woods in themselves were not unusual. The sort of woods you may find in hundreds of places in Oregon or Washington, in fact. However, there was a feeling Jake had about them. Something was very strange about them. As he walked through, he couldn't really sense what it was properly. Except that he felt heavy. Simon too, he noticed was walking slower than he normally did, even though they were both scanning the area for animal sign and tracks, as they normally did.

"Is it just me or are these woods creepy as shit!" Said Simon.

Jake laughed, "Yes, I was thinking the same thing. I was trying to look for a word to describe them. I guess oppressive would do very well. Like they are hanging heavy on your shoulders."

"Well, Rick told me that the path through them wasn't very long," said Jake, "and he was right about that", said Simon, as he pointed to daylight which was now only about 400 feet in front of them.

"Yes, I see it," said Jake, and if that's the case, then this must be the hillside where we aren't supposed to go down, where Rick thinks they might live, in caves."

"Correction," said Simon, he was told in a dream, by the wise ones that that is their home".

"Ah that's it, "said Jake. " Yes."

"Do you want to go down?" Asked Simon.

"Umm not at the moment," replied Jake, 'but I have to say I am sorely tempted. We promised to respect his wishes though, and that's what we will do. Even though I would love to set up some trail cameras near them at the very least".

By now, they had got to the other side of the woods. On this side, there was a gravel track, which appeared to wind its way gradually down the mountainside towards the valley below and the consequent habitation at its bottom. The views from the clearing were gorgeous. Jake and Simon could see for miles, miles of beautiful forest. "For the first time since I have got here, I feel `lighter'. Much better now".

"Yes I agree," said Simon. "It's so very strange."

Again, as soon as they returned back to the forest trail from whence they had just come, the feelings of oppression came. Eventually, they began scanning `The Circle`, to see what they could find. Jake quickly found a compressed patch in the ground, which might have resembled a print. He began searching the ground, looking for more evidence, when Simon immediately began shouting, calling him over.

'Jake, quick, come look I have found a print!" said Simon.

It was unmistakable. The ground was really hard, where it was, baked dry like the sun, it was like concrete. However, a thin layer of dust from a very visible outline of the print that was about 19 inches in length, Jake calculated, before they got out all their equipment to precisely measure it.

Simon had found it at the two o'clock position, about six feet from the edge of `The Circle`.

"It looks very clearly like it is observing us", said Jake. "Its toes are pointing inwards towards the camp".

"Yes, I would agree with you," said Simon.

When the others returned, Simon took Rick over to the print. "Ah yes, another of those", he said in a rather pompous tone. "We have found so many of them; we don't concern ourselves with them anymore."

After the print find, both Jake and Simon were really looking forward to the night's activities.

"Maybe, just maybe, this Rick and his buddies are not crazy at all, and we really will get some evidence of a Bigfoot," said Simon, as he and Jake stood together, in the smoking area.

"Maybe," said Jake "we are going to find out, that's for sure."

The night began with a cacophony of truly terrible music. Rick said the Bigfoots appreciated soothing music. What he played on his phone, was something like elevator music. "It's like torture, joked Simon. Then, almost as if it were rehearsed, Mike Ian and Rick all took up positions at different points in `The Circle`.

Using a clock face as a guide, Rick got the 12 O'clock. Ian the three, and Mike the nine. That left Jake and Simon by themselves in the smoking area. "Remember to check in on us, so we can tell you what is happening," said Rick.

Jake and Simon waited until the others were in position for a good few minutes before they approached them. They started with Rick, who was fixated at the bushes. Rick did not turn to look at them as they approached him. Instead, he continued to look straight ahead. "He is there! Look right in front of you!" Both of them peered in the bushes. Look, the Daddy Bigfoot! He is watching you!"

Jake and Simon looked at each other. Jake could see nothing, but at first, he was taken aback by the vehemence of Rick's assertions. He motioned with his eyes for Simon to follow him. When they were both out of earshot, he said,

"Was it just me, or did you actually see anything?"

"I saw absolutely nothing", said Simon.

"Yes me too. Let's try Ian." Unlike Rick, Ian did acknowledge them: "ah you are just in time, 'he said, "that female Bigfoot that seems to like you Jake, is here. Look, you can see her crawling on her belly down there. She is putting on quite a show." As he spoke, Ian pointed to what looked to Jake like an empty patch of ground, beneath the bush.

"Err, thank you for showing us, Ian," said Jake. Again, he motioned with his eyes to Simon to turn away so they could discuss it.

"Nothing? Said Jake. "Nothing, replied Simon. Lastly, they approached Mike. On their approach, Mike turned to them and said "boys, you are in for a real treat! I have two of the children here, playing! They are so cute! Look, come and see!" He was so excited he giggled as he said this, and patted Simon excitedly on the back as he spoke.

Jake could see that Simon was uncomfortable and that he didn't know what to say.
"Err... Yes great." Was all he could muster in response.

Jake motioned him away again, and they retired to the smoking area.

"What exactly is going on here? Said Jake, it's like crazy town."

"I agree!" Said Simon. "I don't know if we can last out here."

"Well, there is clearly nothing in the damn bushes, but we did find some possible prints today, so let's see what the morning brings, maybe we have some hair samples."

"I agree," said Simon.

Shortly after, the music stopped, and with that, the others said very little as they prepared for bed, almost like they were in some sort of trance, Jake felt. The moment Jake lay down, he felt his heart racing again. He lay on his cot for hours, listening to the others breathe and snore in turn. When the first grey of dawn began to break through the gloom, he immediately fell asleep. Though he had no idea why his body had waited so long to relax, he was very grateful when it finally did so.

The next day was a quiet one, just as Rick had predicted. The only slightly odd thing about it was Simon's strange behavior.

When Jake finally got up, he was greeted by a smiling Simon. "Hey sleepy head ", said Simon, its already after eight, you have enjoyed a lie in, me and the boys have been up since six."

"Ugh, sorry," said Jake "Did anything happen?"

"Not really. Me and the boys have just had breakfast. We saved you some, of course. I slept really well. And you must have too, judging by the fact that you lay in your cot for so long."

Jake reckoned that he must have got two or three hours sleep at most, but Simon's unusual morning grin had unnerved him a little. A gut instinct told him to play along. "Yes sure, I did," said Jake, returning the same grin.

"After you have eaten, we can go and get the gifting bowls. Rick said to wait for you, and of course he is right."

"Great," said Jake. With that, he walked over to the bowls, where he found the others sporting exactly the same smile as Simon. He returned it, but found it difficult. The retrieval of the bowls though, brought out a different result in Jake, because on them he found a single strand of hair.

"Excellent!" Said Jake. Excited by the find. "On the first night!" Exclaimed Rick. "See, I told you they liked you."

"And we still have a few nights to go, so maybe we will get more," said Simon.

"On top of that, nearly all the food has been consumed now, so we are in for a real treat tonight. The more food that is eaten one night the more of them come in on the next night, I find."

"I can't wait!" Said Simon.

The rest of the day was uneventful. Jake was starting to find the atmosphere around camp, with the other's grinning constantly, almost unbearable. So, he decided to excuse himself by saying he needed to go for a walk and make a phone call in the process. Nobody questioned him about it, or offered to come with him, and that suited him perfectly.

He headed straight out through the woods, marching as quickly as he could. When he got to the other side, he opened his eyes and breathed! The air felt clean, he noticed. The air in `The Circle` felt sickly and oppressive. Like he couldn't breathe. As the sun was shining, he decided to stay. He had two more nights to stick out. He could do that. Rick was going into town again, and he had asked him to buy a load of red bulls as well as the coffee. As he wasn't driving, he reckoned he could keep awake for forty-eight hours. In fact, he needed to. Maybe grab some sleep in the daylight. Really, he wanted to leave. A potential Bigfoot hair sample though, was so tempting. It was worth sticking it out, just for that. Although Simon's strange behavior that morning had worried him.

He decided to rest where he was for a little while. To take a break. Before he knew it, the little while had become a few hours. He decided he couldn't leave Simon there any longer. So, he returned to camp.

Upon his approach, he noticed the other's still adopting the same irritating grin. He returned it as best he could, for he had a feeling that challenging them would be a bad idea. However, the rest of the day was unremarkable and this allowed Jake to relax a little.

It was only when night began to fall, that he felt himself tense. Tonight though, it was almost a full moon, and he was grateful for the light it afforded. It felt comforting, particularly in this place. Just as it was getting dark, Ian and Rick beckoned Jake and Simon over to the trunk of Ian's car, where they were both standing.

"Now you are both one of us, we wanted to show you this," said Rick. By now, Ian had opened up the car trunk, and in it was a machine. It was about three feet wide, by three feet in length. On it, was copper wire, and three crystals, which looked like amethysts, were connected to a battery.

"What is it?" said Jake.

"It came to me in a dream that this was the way forward," said Rick. "This was what I needed to do. You see these Bigfoots are not from our world. They needed our help, and they asked me to build this. I am not a technical man though. So I asked Ian, and he obliged."

Jake was ready for the night when it came. The guys spread out into their now familiar place, with the same dreadful music.

As before, Jake and Simon went over to Rick first. He was again staring intently into the woods. "Can you see him?" said Rick."

"The Daddy Bigfoot. He is there, just in front of us."

"I can see him now yes!" Said Simon excitedly. "Wow, he must be like ten feet tall!"

"Can you see him, Jake?" Said Simon.

"Err, yes I can, I can see him, wonderful!" Jake lied. For he could see nothing at all, just like before .The other two seemed unperturbed by Jake's obviously bad acting, and continued with their excited chatter, about the `Daddy Bigfoot`.

Jake eventually managed to pull Simon away from Rick and guided him towards Mike. Again, Mike reported seeing the `children playing `. Again, unlike last night, Simon could see them. Finally, they approached Ian. Ian had the same belly crawling female Bigfoot, in front of him. Again, Simon could see this creature, while all Jake had seen in all of these places was the same empty forest. Simon on the other hand, darted amongst them excitedly.

Eventually, the music stopped, and the others began preparing for bed.

Jake decided he had to try and reach Simon, to try and get to him before he tried to go to sleep again. So, under the pretense of asking him if he would like to join him for a cigarette, he took Simon over to the smoking area, while the others began lying down.

"Simon," said Jake, "can you really see those things or are you just humoring them?" Simon seemed puzzled even by the question, and frowned as he replied,

"Of course I can see them! Why, can't you, Jake?"

"I was just pretending to keep them happy like we did last night," said Jake. "I can't really see anything."

"Really? Wow!" Replied Simon. "They are everywhere!"

"Simon, they are **not** everywhere!" By now, Jake had grabbed Simon's arm in his earnestness to convince his friend "Last night, we saw nothing! Nothing at all! That's because there was nothing. Tonight, there is nothing!"

"Well how can you explain my reaction then?"

"I can't! I don't know. I…."

It was at that point that Jake noticed a beam of light across the pathway in front of him. He was by now hypervigilant, looking out for anything odd, and he could see that this was not moonlight. It was too defined, sharp and pointed. It was like a beam. About 70 yards down the path.

"Are you guys coming to bed?" Rick shouted down to them.

"Oh you go on, we are just having a cigarette, and we will catch up with you in the morning!" Jake shouted back in reply.

"I am going to go too, "said Simon yawning.
" I am really tired."

"No, please wait. Just a little while." Said Jake. Just ten minutes. There is something not right about the appearance of that light. I want to see what happens with it."

"Okay Jake," I will wait. Simon was reluctant, but he indulged his friend, at least with one final cigarette before bed.

The only had to wait less than a minute though, before a crackling sound began to emit from the beam of light. Then sparks of different colors shot off it, before it stabilized into a form of red mist.

"What is going on?" Said Simon, by now alarmed at what he was seeing.

"I have no idea whatsoever," said Jake very slowly, he began slowly pausing over each word now.

It was at that point that the two men were about to have the strangest moment of their lives though. For as they stood watching, they saw two figures emerge from the mist. Jake's first thought was that they did not appear `natural`. Although he could not articulate it into speech at the time. The creatures were small, no taller than three feet. They were jet black, with small pointed red eyes. Jake could clearly see that they had two arms and two legs, but no other features were discernable. No mouth, nose or ears were visible. They had what he would later describe as a robust physique, stocky and strong looking. They were both surrounded by a ragged orange light, which glowed slightly. They did not emerge from it. Rather, they stayed there staring at them, while Jake and Simon returned the stare, completely astounded at what they were both seeing.

"What the hell are they?" said Simon. He did not take his eyes off the creatures as he spoke.

"I have no idea," said Jake. "I want to be clear though. Simon, please can you describe to me exactly what you are seeing. I want to be very sure that I am not hallucinating, and that we are seeing the same thing."

"I can see two small figures about three foot tall, black, hovering in a sort of raggedy orange glow." Said Simon.

"Do the creatures you see have red eyes, like pinpoints?" Said Jake.

"Yes, yes they do," replied Simon. "Well then,' said Jake, we are seeing the same thing. Exactly. That's amazing!"

"What are we going to do about it, about them?"

"Well, the first thing we are going to do, is ask Rick about them, replied Jake, because as I very clearly recall, Rick talked a lot, but he never mentioned anything like this to me".

"Or to me, "said Simon.

With that, Jake ran over to the cots, where the others were by now fast asleep. It took a while to wake them, but shouting eventually did the trick.

"Rick, I need you to come immediately please! And you too Ian and Mike, I want you to come with us right now!"

The urgency in Jake's voice invited no contradiction of what by now was a command, and the others threw off their blankets and silently walked the short distance to where Jake made them stand. The creatures hadn't moved. They still stood there, hovering. As if they were waiting for something to happen.

"I want you to tell me what you see please, Rick."

"I see two little black creatures standing there. Really strange. In an odd orange light."

"Yes, and they have odd red eyes," added Ian.

"I see the same thing," said Mike.

"This is so very strange," said Jake "those creatures should not exist in nature, yet they do. There is no species anything like them, obviously. Yet here they are." I have never seen anything like them. Can you tell me what they are, Rick? Have you ever seen them before?"

"I have absolutely no idea," replied Rick. "You are not welcome here!" he shouted at the creatures. The creatures did not respond and continued to just hover by the strange red mist.

The moment Rick shouted though, Jake saw that his body slumped, and he immediately looked exhausted. Ian and Mike did exactly the same thing. Almost like dolls that had just had their batteries taken out of them.

Rick then turned to Jake and said, "I am exhausted, I think we should go to bed."

"I agree." Said Ian.

"You are actually joking! Two creatures that nobody has ever seen before suddenly appear, and you guys want to go to bed!"

Rick made no response to this, he just shrugged his shoulders and began walking off. Ian followed. Only Simon lingered for a few seconds, before, he too, fell into line behind the others.

"Please tell me you are not going to bed too," said Jake to Simon

"I can't explain it, I feel strangely tired, but I am fighting it, "said Simon, "get me a red bull!"

"I will get us both one!" Exclaimed Jake.

They both stood there then, watching the creatures. The creatures still hadn't moved. They still continued to hover.

"It's like they are waiting for something," said Jake.

"Waiting for what though?" Replied Simon.

"I don't know. All I can say is that they are not hallucinations, as we have described their physical appearance to each other. I am certain though that there is no way I am going to bed with these things around. We have no idea what they are here for, or what will happen if we do go to sleep and are left vulnerable to them."

"Damn these things!" Said Simon.

Then, he shouted angrily down the track to where the creatures were still hovering "what are you going to do if we don't go to bed then, eh?"

The moment that Simon said this, the creatures came angrily charging down the path, towards them, still immersed in the orange glow.

One was headed straight for Jake, while the other had veered off toward Simon. In his horror, Jake realized that he might die here. No one would find his body or ever understand what had happened to him. He and Simon would just be another mystery disappearance case, and there were thousands of them every year. No trace of them would ever be found. With the creature destined for him now just ten yards or from him, Jake readied to fight it. Should he kick it, punch it or what? He resolved to kick it first. Now he could see that it did in fact have a mouth, and it was twisted into an angry hateful snarl, as it rushed straight at him. Jake remembered his head torch, and as he steadied himself to kick the creature, he switched it on, with his right hand, all the time keeping the creature directly in his line of vision.

The moment he did so, the creature vanished! As did the one seemingly destined for Simon. The mist and everything with it, was also gone!

"What just happened?" Said an incredulous Simon.

"Everything has vanished!"

"Yes it is like nothing ever happened, there is no trace of them," replied Jake. "It is like the flashlight did something to them."

"We must wake the others then," said Simon. "In case those things come back."

"I agree," said Jake. They tried as hard as they could, even physically shaking them, but they were totally unsuccessful in doing so.

"It's like they are in a coma, or something like it, " said Simon.

Then, the beam of light appeared in the path, and the crackling started again, with lights sparking in all directions, like tiny fireworks. The two friends watched in horror as the red mist also appeared again.

"Quick!" Said Jake, and he turned on his flashlight, pointing the beam directly at the mist.

This time, Simon did exactly the same thing. Whoosh! The mist instantly disappeared, just like it had never been there.

"What is happening here?" Said Simon.

"I have no idea, I just know that we have to keep this going until daylight" said Jake.

And they did. Each time the mist formed, they flashed their headlights at it, and each time they did, it vanished in response.

Eventually, with dawn breaking, they collapsed exhausted onto their respective cots, and joined in the others in much needed sleep.

It was 7.30 am when Rick woke them. By his own groggy calculation, Jake had not been asleep for much more than an hour.

"Good morning gentlemen," said Rick. "Mike has prepared some breakfast."

"Are you ready to go and check on the gifting bowls soon?"

"Erm yes, yes we are. First though, I want to talk about those creatures we saw last night," said Jake.

"All in good time. Get something to eat first. You both look very tired today. Then we can grab the bowls, and then talk about what we saw. Okay?" Rick was very direct and assertive in the way he spoke, especially when he was trying to be persuasive.

"Okay," said Jake. He realized that he was starving hungry.

"I am good with that," said Simon, nodding his head.

Jake chewed his breakfast reluctantly. Although he was hungry, this morning food was purely functional to him rather than enjoyable.

After that, they headed off to the bowls. As he began examining them, Rick began to get very excited.

The food contained within them had been greedily consumed. As well as the usual donuts and Cheetos, Rick had placed four peanut butter and jelly sandwiches. Not a trace remained. "See, a wild animal could not do this", he said. "They are sophisticated."

It was the four hairs smeared in the jam on the outside rim of the bowl, which particularly excited Rick though.

"There you are, Jake," he said. "Now you are good to go on the hairs. Hopefully we can grab a few more for comparison purposes after we spend our final night here."

"Hopefully yes," said Jake. Jake was deliberately non-committal and guarded in what he said to Rick now. He understood that the next twenty-four hours would be critical.

When they got back to camp, Ian and Mike were waiting for them smiling. Rick bade Simon and Jake sit opposite him on their cots while he spoke.

"Last night was certainly very unusual. I want you to know, but in a good way. When I went back to sleep, the Bigfoot people spoke to me in a dream. They told me how the two beings that we saw are not there to attack us. They are in fact, `guardians of the portal`. That red mist you saw was energy to another world. The place where they come from. The beings that manifested here have a job which is to guard the gate, to make sure nobody that shouldn't, comes through it. We would not survive for long in their world, like they can in ours. They are here to help us after that, in my dream, I saw a being of pure love."

"Rick, these things attacked us! They disappeared when we shot a light directly at them!" Said Jake, who was getting frustrated, despite his attempt to keep calm.

Rick smiled at this and replied, "do not worry, Jake. They are not here to do anything else but help. Trust me." Rick laid his hand on Jake's leg as he said this.

"I saw this too," said Ian. "We are blessed by these people."

Jake noticed that Mike stayed quiet. He still had the same grin on his face that he always did, it just looked slightly more strained than normal.

"What I would like for you two guys is rest up here today, if that's alright. We are going to get some treats in town and some good surprises for tonight, okay? " Said Rick.

"In the meantime, you guys can just relax and enjoy yourselves here."

"Okay" said Simon. It was one of the only words he had spoken since they were awake.

Jake and Simon watched the other's drive away. Neither of them protested. They both wanted and needed to talk.

"What actually happened last night?" Said Simon. It actually feels like a very bizarre dream."

"Yes, it really does," said Jake "except it isn't. Those creatures were real! It was real that they attacked us! Whatever **they** are, they are not `guardians` of anything. Why would creatures that are nine feet tall, alleged Bigfoots, need to have these things that are three feet tall acting as guardians? Also , they have technology that is way beyond ours , why would they have to resort to eating old donuts from a bowl. That explanation is just nonsense and way too convenient."

"I agree," said Simon. "The whole thing was bizarre and horrific at the same time. Well, we can just hike out of here right now, if you want? I reckon we can just follow the trail down the hillside, and eventually we will get to a road. It can't be more than a few hours."

"No, I want to, but I don't want to, if that makes sense," said Jake. "I want to leave, because that was a terrible experience, but I want to stay as well, because it was also truly amazing, and I want to reaffirm what I saw, to be sure."

'Well, we saw them for hours, not just a glimpse, and so I am very sure they exist. I take your point though about wanting to have it affirmed though. And the business with the flashlights? That was strange on top of strange," said Simon.

"Yes, I agree, it was like they were a weapon, like they we were shooting."

"That's exactly what we were doing, "said Jake. "They have superior technology to us, but it has limits, and that is their vulnerability. I think we can get through another night because we have them."

"What if we can't though, and they have figured a way around it?" said Simon.

"Then we are probably in a lot of trouble. I don't buy any of Rick's stories at all. I think he is driven by ego, and those things know it. They are his dear friends, and he their trusted ambassador, yet they won't even show themselves to him? Have you noticed how they are always in the shadows, just out of reach? And the weird emphasis on sleep? Neither of us could see them the first night, but after that, when you slept well, you began to see them." Said Jake.

"Yes, that's true," said Simon. "So, what do you want to do?"

First of all, I want to examine the area where they appeared, and see if there is any way they could have faked it, for example with projectors, or in the alternative ,if there is any evidence of any technology used." Jake replied.

"You don't believe Rick faked this do you? Said Simon.

"I mean I wish he had, that would make life so much easier for both of us. It just doesn't fit his narrative though. He wants us to like it here. Its good publicity for him."

"Yes, and he has now created a new story around these creatures which will satisfy his ever growing army of followers. Look, we were not meant to see these things last night, they were waiting for something. I think they were waiting for us to go to sleep. It actually makes me disturbed thinking what might have happened to us on the first night when we both did go to sleep."

"Maybe nothing." Said Simon. "Rick did say that it takes them a while to get going."

"Maybe," said Jake. "The big question thought is what do they want? They want something, that's clear. I just don't know what yet. I can't work it out just yet. Maybe tonight will give us some answers."

"I hope so, "said Simon. " Well, we had better get started then. I would like to do the inspection, and then get some rest, if that's okay?"

"Yes, me too," said Jake.
Firstly, they inspected the pathway where both the strange mist and the creatures appeared. Then, they looked either side of the road for any evidence of any machinery, or even for any indication something had been placed there, liked scuff marks for example. There was nothing.

They took comparison photos of themselves standing in the same place as the creatures had for later comparison purposes, and then scoured all around `The Circle`, for any additional evidence of the creatures. There was nothing. Nothing at all anywhere.

"It's like they never existed, there is no trace of them anywhere," said Simon.

"Yes, 'that's exactly what they want, they are thorough," replied Jake.

He and Simon both lay down on the cots after that. While Simon went quickly to sleep though, Jake found that he was unable to do so. Eventually, he decided to wander to the other side of the woods. The atmosphere in `The Circle`, had become increasingly oppressive to him, especially when the creatures appeared.

He crossed the woods, which today seemed gloomy and melancholic in nature. The moment he did so, he sucked the fresh air into his lungs, and breathed hard. The air felt fresh and sweet.

He had no desire to go back now. Part of him just wanted to start walking on the trail down to the main road. He would never do that of course. He wouldn't leave Simon for one thing. He did close his eyes though and allowed himself the luxury of some sweet sleep…

When he awoke, he felt a little energized. He steadied himself mentally, to prepare himself for the obvious rigors of the day ahead. Before he had left, he had told Simon that he may walk to the other side of the woods if he couldn't sleep, as he didn't want to cause him any extra unnecessary worry. Poor Simon, Jake thought. The strain on his face was really evident. Yet if it was on Simon's face, what did his face also look like?

The sooner they both go out of this place the better, he thought.

When he emerged from the woods into `The Circle`, he could see the other's had returned and were unpacking stuff, so they hadn't been back long. With them, was a boy, who Jake guessed must be about 11 or 12 years old.

Rick was the first to see Jake emerge from the woods. As he approached, Rick said "Ah you are back! Jake, allow me to introduce my son. Jake this is Jimmy. Jimmy, this is Jake"

Jimmy stuck out his hand awkwardly and approached Jake.

"Pleased to meet you, sir," he said.

Jake shook his hand "And you too Jimmy. Just call me Jake. Jake is fine".

Then Jake turned to Rick and said: "Rick I would really like a word with you please, if that's okay?"

"Of course, "Rick replied smoothly.

"Now is a good time," said Jake, "and away from the group please."

"Of course," said Rick. With that, Jake walked to the six o'clock position in `The Circle`. On arriving, Jake turned to Rick and said, "tell me exactly what has made you think it was a good idea to invite a child here? You know what we saw last night, Rick!"

"I do know! Said Rick, jabbing a finger excitedly in the air as he did so. I know exactly what happened! The problem is that you don't know, my dear boy!"

"Last night, I will admit that what I saw troubled me. Then, just as I was saying to your friend Simon, I had another dream, a new revelation! The Bigfeet visited me in a dream! They told me that those creatures are guardians! They are guarding a portal into another world where all the Bigfeet live. They are making sure nobody crosses over that shouldn't! We are helping to save them, don't you see? Ian's machine is strengthening the link between our world and theirs. Soon, they will be able to cross over without it. When they do, they will be able to reveal themselves to us all .It will be wonderful!"

"Rick, you are entitled to believe what you want, that's your choice, but personally speaking, I think it's a great mistake for your to bring your child into this," said Jake. "I don't mind being wrong. I really don't. You however, must entertain the possibility that you MIGHT be ".

"Now Jake," replied Rick, a little more forcefully this time, "I understand that you are a little disturbed by what you saw, but I am telling you that this is the truth. The guardians are just pure love. In any event, no doubt you and Simon will be staying up all night, so you can protect us if you feel that is necessary."

With that, Rick turned on his heels and returned to the others, indicating very clearly that the matter was closed. Jake was of course fuming, but he knew nothing further was to be said. He stood there smoking a cigarette, getting ready for the night.

Simon came over to join him, and this time he was joined by a nervous looking Mike. "Not happy about the kid joining us eh? Said Simon. "I guess that's what your conversation with Rick was about?"

"Not happy about it is an understatement. We can't exactly leave here now, it's about to get dark, and those trails would be treacherous at night". Said Jake.

'No, we have to stick it out for the night, mate." Replied Simon.

"Did he tell you that story about how they visited him in a dream, and how they are `guardians´ or some such nonsense. Now Jake turned to Mike and said. "Mike, how could creatures that grow up to ten feet tall need something three feet to guard their `portal` for them? And if they are capable of technology way beyond anything humanity possesses, then why are any of them after Rick's moldy old donuts?"

At this, Simon and even Mike laughed. "Look, Mike I know you are really good friends with Rick, and I am sorry I am denigrating him in front of you, I just think it is extremely foolhardy him bringing his son here."

Then Simon said, "Mike has something he wants to tell you, Jake. He pulled me to one side when they all arrived back to camp.

"Yes," said Mike nervously, "when I first came to `*The Circle*`, the first night I was here, I was going to sleep, and then I felt a tremendous pain in my leg, as I awoke in a start, I saw a creature. Huge it was, with a face like a wolf. It was standing over me. It had bright red eyes, and its teeth! They were like nothing I have ever seen! Then I went back to sleep, and it was like it never happened. When I woke up the next day I felt great."

"Does Rick know about this?" Said Jake.

"Yes, Rick knows. He told me not to tell anyone though."

"He told you not to tell anyone!" Jake exclaimed angrily. "He only wants information released that fits his narrative!"

Mike said nothing in response. He then pulled a large revolver from the backpack he was carrying. "I want you to have this for the night, Jake. I may fall asleep, I know I might. If anything comes, I want you to be ready. It's loaded."

"Thank you Mike". Jake calmed at this, grateful for the gift.

"Well, we had better get on with the evening then guys," he said.

The three men walked over to the others now, who were busy laying out the table.

"Guys, I told you I have a surprise for you," beamed Rick. "Tonight, as a special treat I have bent my rules and brought some alcohol! Yayy! I didn't know what you guys wanted, so I have brought beer and wine. There is even whisky and vodka, and some mixers if you want it? As for me, I am having some beer with my burgers."

Jake smiled very calmly. "I will have some red wine please," he said.

"That's an excellent choice, I have some Merlot which I hope is to your liking. Ian, will you play barkeep please?"

"Of course," said Ian, "it will be my pleasure."

Simon asked for a beer, which was duly handed to him by the ever-smiling Ian.

They exchanged pleasantries with the others for a few minutes, before Jake drew Simon away to the place where they were permitted to smoke, under the pretense of needing a cigarette.

"Don't drink it, " said Jake to Simon.

"What?" said Simon. Are you kidding me? Its free booze!"

"Don't you see?" Said Jake. "Look at all this food! Burgers, pizzas, endless alcohol of many kinds! Rick, or rather whatever is really influencing and in control of him, wants us to have all of this! And you know why? I will tell you why! So that we sleep! It's all about us going to sleep! Then, those damn horrible things will attack us, and drag us through their portal. Or experiment on us, or whatever they have planned. Whatever it is, it isn't good!"

"Yes of course, you are right! They will attack us! The booze and food are meant to send us to sleep!" Said Simon.

"Just pretend you are drinking it, play along with them, you can pour it in the bushes when we are here, smoking. It's too dark for them to see us doing that, if we are careful about it."

"I will, "said Simon. "Okay then, let's join them for the party, and let's see what happens," said Jake, and they walked back to join the others.

"Before the party begins, I am going to let Jimmy give a quick call to his mum. I know the cellphone signal is really bad here, even at the best of times, and you guys have not been able to make a call yet. Would you like to make one before he does?"

"That's very kind of you, but I can wait until the morning," said Jake.

"I am good too." Replied Simon.

Jimmy's call to his mother was short, lasting only a minute or two. At the end of it, Jimmy said, "I love you Mum, goodbye."

"The kid's just said goodbye to his Mum, we are all going to die," quipped Simon. Jake laughed out loud at this evidently dark humor. The first real laugh he had had in ages.

Then the dreadful music began. Ian, Mike and Rick all adopted their usual stances. At first, Jimmy seemed nervous, but he held his Dad's hand as he animatedly pointed out imaginary Bigfoot's in the bushes. Jake could see him nodding his head, so presumably he had got into it too.

Jake also bade Simon stay with him this time. "Sleep seemed to affect you last time, you got sucked into it. I want you to keep your wits about you this time. So please just stay with me and wait it out until they have gone to bed. We are going to need everything we have to fight these things."

"I totally agree, "said Simon. I am going to stay right here until they all go to bed".

The night followed an exact pattern to the previous ones. Rick, Mike and Ian, were transfixed by what was in the bushes, as was Jimmy now too. Eventually, Rick turned off the music. With that, they all retired to their cots, almost like it was a drill. They barely acknowledged Simon and Jake as they did do.

Jake and Simon pulled up some camper chairs and waited.

On cue, a beam of vertical light shot across the path.

"Now it begins," said Jake. He and Simon tensed for the battle that was surely to come.

The crackling began, shooting out like fireworks into the night. Then came the red mist. The instant it started to form, Jake and Simon both shot their flashlights out at it, and it instantly disappeared. "These things are like guns to it," said Simon.

"Exactly," said Jake. "We need to hold them off until daybreak."

Jake had the presence of mind to take a photo, just in case they were engulfed, and somebody found their bodies. He also timed how long it took for the whole `Portal`, if that is what it was, took to appear. About six minutes, from the moment the beam appeared, to the complete materialization. Adrenaline and determination kept them both going.

Jake knew all he had to do was keep going until daylight.

He pushed himself and focused. Suddenly, just twenty minutes before dawn, there was a sudden surge in activity, Jake fired his beam, but the mist did not retreat. Rather it cleared. Looking through it, Jake could see what looked like a view. A view with a red sky and barren hills. He could also see a twisted tree. It had no leaves on it. It looked exhausted, the way vegetation looks in New England in January. The creatures were by it. Waiting. Only there were many more of them this time.

"Simon! Simon!" Jake shouted. He had looked across at his friend, and saw that he had fallen into an exhausted sleep. "They got to you, made you sleep! Wake up!"

Simon awoke with a start, and automatically reached for his light. As soon as he fired it, the mist and everything in it disappeared.

When daybreak finally came, Jake felt like it was one of the greatest moments of his life. The two men climbed onto their cots truly exhausted by their activities.

An hour later, they were shook awake by Rick, who offered them a breakfast, again cooked by the ever dutiful Mike. The subsequent trip to the gifting bowls proved even more rewarding than the first two trips, generating as it did some substantial strands of hair, which Jake duly tagged and bagged.

"I hope you have all you need to extract the DNA, "said Rick.

"I hope so too," said Jake, "but we will have to see what the Professor says."

"Of course," said Rick. "I will be very curious."


After breakfast, they said goodbye to Ian and Mike, and dropped Jimmy off at Rick's first wife's house, which was only about an hour from the site of `The Circle.`

They hadn't talked at all about what happened until they stopped for lunch. Ian and Mike had wanted to press on, but Jake was glad of the stop. He was suddenly starving.

"I wonder if you wouldn't mind doing me a favor when we stop gentlemen when we stop. Please could you recount your activities in `The Circle`, for people on film. I am sure everyone would find it interesting," said Rick.

Jake had been anticipating this and responded straightaway "I want to be very clear Rick. We CANNOT talk about those creatures that appeared in the red mist. We fundamentally disagree on what they are, as well. We also have no evidence of them and it will just look like a crazy story."

"I agree with Rick," said Simon, "I don't mind saying that there was activity in `*The Circle*`, but I am not going to say that there was anything like those creatures. I would look crazy, I could well lose my job if it went public."

"Of course, my friends," said Rick smiling warmly," no problem at all. We will just confine it to the video, and I promise to say nothing at all about the guardians until we all agree to talk about them."

With the video made, and lunch greedily consumed, both Simon and Jake fell asleep almost immediately when they got back into Rick's car. In fact, they hardly spoke at all until they said goodbye to him. Rick was oblivious to this of course, and did more than enough talking for the three of them.

Philip was waiting for them at the airport when they arrived. He was surprised to see how disheveled and exhausted his friends both looked, after less than a week away. "You look like you have just spent a month in the jungle! He exclaimed "What in the hell happened to you two?"

"Take us to a bar." Said Jake.

"I want to drink and drink." Said Simon.

And they did.

Jake hadn't puked his guts out over booze since he was a teenager, when he had hold of his Dad's whisky. He did the next morning though. And although it made him feel better, he was also faced with the terrible realization that he felt he felt compelled to return….

# Chapter Six

## Darkness Rising

Marybelle had been really looking forward to showing Mike what happened at the tree. They had been on a few dates now. He seemed really nice. He was stable. He had a very good job and a house. He didn't have a lot of emotional baggage. Nothing like her issues anyway. And he didn't have the bad she debts that she had. So, he would be perfect, she reckoned. First, she would show him the tree, scare him a little, and show him her crazy. If he could cope with that. Well, she would let him look after her. He would be lucky, she thought, I am hot. Not as hot as I used to be, a bit plumper, that was certainly true, but still looking good. Still a catch….

The Jinn was bored. He had been stuck in this place for three hundred years now. Banished from Iblis's presence for his disobedience. His powers were also limited. He could barely leave his prison under the tree. When he did, it was normally an exhausting effort. He was so frustrated. He had no power at all to make mischief, to torment the humans. That was what gave him true pleasure. He was just stuck here. A prisoner. Miserable.

Then this woman had come along, and he had found himself able to communicate with her. Bumps and thuds. She had thought him stupid and left him ridiculous trinkets. Her own intellect if that was the right word for it was nothing next to his.

Over time, his ability to connect with her had grown stronger. He wondered if he could do actually do *it* now. He would try. What had he to lose?

"I am just going to go around the other side of the tree to stomp there, Mike." Okay?
"Okay Marybelle," said Mike, who was at first bemused by the whole thing, but then surprised at the bumps back that she had been receiving.

"Hey big guy! She said in an affected yet sweet voice like she was talking to a child "are you going to bump for me?"

It was at that point that the Jinn struck, launching himself from the ground, he grabbed the woman, wrapping himself around her, which enabled him to materialize her back into the ground. It was all so quick that Marybelle did not even have time to speak.

"Marybelle? Marybelle?" Called Mike, in an ever increasing desperation.

He didn't find Marybelle though. Nor did the search parties. They even dug under the tree, but found nothing. For The Jinn had taken her far far below to his lair. "When you have stopped screaming, you can clean the fish," he said to Marybelle, tossing her a salmon.

She was mortal of course, she would not last forever. Now he had her though, he could extend her life for a few hundred years of course. If she behaved herself. Time would tell...

The Perkins had never really been an adventurous couple. Mr. Perkins had done moderately well, as a middle manager. They had lived in a comfortable house in a suburb of Seattle, since they were married in 1995. Mrs. Perkins had only had one boyfriend and one very intimate sexual experience with another man, before she met `her Chad. 'They didn't travel much. They had no children and no pets. Between them, they only had one elderly parent left, Mr. Perkins mother. She was in her eighties and practically senile though. She could barely even recognize her own son. They were like millions of other people. They had done nothing wrong. They had just got through life with each other. So, when Chad told her they were going to spend their annual vocation on a drive down to Oregon, and even stay in some fancy hotels for at least part of the time, Mrs. Perkins was understandably delighted. Chad never usually suggested anything adventurous. Normally they had those irritating `staycations` which basically consisted of him lying around the house watching sports, while her life went on as a normal. Occasionally though, they had rented a cabin for the weekend on the Olympic peninsula. That was always lovely. However, a whole two week vacation was a real treat.

    They had spent the first night in the Hoh rainforest. Mrs. Perkins had just loved it, all the wonderful nature. They hadn't walked about much though, for neither of them were really dressed for it, and it started raining .They had however walked long enough for it to take her breath away .It was such an ancient place .And the air was so pure. It was wonderful. She was so happy.

    The drive down through Oregon had proved to be really enjoyable too. Mrs. Perkins loved connecting with nature, and now especially, she felt the optimism of early spring. They had stopped a few times, to look at the views and once at a vineyard, so, as a consequence, they drove into the town where their hotel was, quite a bit later than they intended. Chad was behaving a little strangely to on the way down, he seemed confused. In fact, she nearly took over the driving. As they drove into Bend, though, she noticed that all the streetlights were out "Do you think they have had a power cut, Chad?" said Mrs. Perkins.

" I don't know, Mary," he replied. "My G.P.S. doesn't seem to be working either. I reckon I can still find the Hotel though. Their website said it was right in the middle of town. The Pilot Butte Inn is its name. Look out for it when we get there."

Navigation around the town was remarkably easy though. Even though it was only eight pm, there was no traffic on the roads. "There it is! Exclaimed Mrs. Perkins excitedly! Right in the middle of town, just as you said. "Yes, well done Mary, replied Mr. Perkins. "I can't find the parking though. It was supposed to be right at the front of their Hotel."

"Well, I guess you can just park there, at the front anyway. "Said Mary. "It doesn't look like there are any restrictions?"

'I guess not," said Mr. Perkins, shrugging his shoulders.

The moment they parked their car, a man from the hotel instantly appeared to greet them. He was dressed in a 19th Century bell hop uniform.

"Good evening." He said. "May I ask your name?"

"We are Mr. and Mrs. Perkins."

"Very good sir, may I take your bags?"

"Of course, thank you." Said Chad.

The bell boy directed them to the check in where a man stood immaculate in a pinstriped suit and waistcoat. He had slicked back hair. "My name is Chalmers, he announced as they checked in. And I will help you with all of your needs. Here is you room key, sir. He handed Mr. Perkins an old fashioned brass door key. "Breakfast begins from 6 am. Goodnight".

The bell hop showed them to their room. The furniture seemed antique, and Mrs. Perkins thought that she rather liked the look.

There was no TV in the room, and no facilities for making coffee, which was a little odd. Still, the bell hop had seemed delighted with the two dollar tip he had had got from Chad, even though she had considered it a little mean. Chad would of course say that he was being `careful`. He had always been `careful`.

Mrs. Perkins found the décor amazing though, and when she had asked her husband if they could spend another night there, he hadn't refused.

"Did you see the charges for room service and the Hotel charge. It's incredibly cheap here, said Mr. Perkins. "I may even look for a job around here. Do you fancy moving to Oregon, my love?"

"Ohh yes that would be wonderful, I would love it!" She had never heard him be so adventurous.'' We could look tomorrow."

They both slept very heavily that night. In fact, Mrs. Perkins couldn't remember a time when she had slept so well in years. She awoke refreshed and they both happily headed downstairs. She veered off to the breakfast room, while her husband went straight to reception to speak with the manager, it was the same man from last night.

He must work very long shifts, thought Mrs. Perkins to herself.

She studied the breakfast menu while she waited for her husband. They had got up early, so there were only a few guests peppering the breakfast room. They all were dressed in suits, so she concluded that a lot of business must stay in the Hotel. She had more important matters to tend to though. She was exceptionally hungry, and she hadn't had pancakes in ages...

Mr. Perkins came bounding in just a few minutes later, clutching a newspaper that was on the desk.

"I was talking to that guy Chalmers on reception, about job opportunities around here. I was asking him if he had any leads with companies around here, after I checked us in for another night. And now I know why everything is so cheap around here. Do you know how much that guy earns as a hotel manager? He was every open about it, I didn't ask him. Eleven thousand dollars a year! As a hotel manager! I am sorry sweetheart, but we are not moving here. The place looks old fashioned and beautiful, but the wages suck."

"That doesn't make sense though," said Mary, who was by now starting to feel very anxious. "We are only in Oregon. We are not in a poor country on the other side of the world."

Then she paused. As if her mind was making horrifying connections.

Now, she spoke very slowly to her husband:

"Show me the paper Chad."

"What?" He replied.

"Show me the paper." He looked at her with a puzzled expression before folding it again. "What does it say? "She pressed the point.

"Oh, it can't be a real newspaper," he replied, "it must be one of those novelty ones or something. The headline says that we just declared war on Germany for goodness sake!

"Hand it me quick!" She grabbed the paper from him. "This paper is dated April 7$^{th}$, 1917!"

"So?" He replied!

"Remember, she said "I was a history major. This is the day AFTER Congress voted to declare war on Germany."

"So?" he replied incredulously. "This is April 2023, not April 2017."

'What if it isn't though, Chad? What if we are here NOW in 1917? Think about it! The prices, the Hotel, the lack of computers. Everything!"

"That's just an insane theory! "He scoffed.

"Is it really?" She replied. I think we could be in some kind of time slip. We could be in the past!"

"I don't think-" .Mr. Perkins never finished his reply.

Suddenly, two figures appeared at their table. Both were armed, and they appeared to be wearing an old-fashioned military uniform.

"Mr. and Mrs. Perkins, I am arresting you on suspicion of being German spies".

"No" said Mrs. Perkins, holding her hand to her mouth.

"This is preposterous!" Said Mr. Perkins, who eventually had to be dragged to his cell shouting.

The Perkins had left no trace in the present. Now though, they had left a very definite one in the past.

Juan was excited. He was now twelve years old, and today everyone had gathered for his birthday. He thought he was getting a bit old for the piñata, but he would indulge his parents. Plus, there were added benefits as well. After it had been demolished, he would move in for just a little kiss on the cheek with Theresa. Theresa had been his crush since he was eight years old, and he was ready to act. In order to achieve his goal, Juan knew though that he had to look cool. So, he had been secretly practicing for months now. He had put his own blindfold on and grabbed a stick. He had tied an old pillow to the tree where the piñata was due to be hung. He had even worked out the approximate height that it would be placed at. Then, once everything was in place, he had imagined himself as a Jedi warrior, learning the ways of the force, making himself ready. Juan knew that it took years of training to become a true Jedi. He didn't have years of training, though. He was only going to have a few months. However, if he was going to win the hand of Princess Theresa, then he would and could do this. He knew it.

He knew now to listen to the creak in the rope. That was when the Piñata would swing in. He also knew the weight of the stick. He had practiced striking the tree and learnt how to position his lower body to give maximum thrust and power to the blows. In order to look especially good, he was going to have to open it up in three blows. One was almost impossible, two extremely unlikely. Three was just possible. If he was really really good.

He had also planned it so that his older brother's would go first. Of course, as the birthday boy that was his right. He would allow it though. His parents would question this, but he would just look reasonable and generous. His brother's greed would win them over and Antonio and Jose would both try and fail. The odds were stacked against them. Then he would go up. Use his three blows, and bang! Victory would be all the sweeter, as it would also be a victory over them.

It was important that his parents selected the traditional piñata, the donkey. The natural instinct his brothers, and everyone else had, was to aim for the head or the body. They would be blindfolded of course, so this was the biggest surface area. Yet, if you wanted it to break open that was a big mistake. The weakest point he reckoned, was the right leg. If he could concentrate on just that point, with three blows, he reckoned he could burst it open. Of course, you would have to practice with a blindfold on to achieve this goal, but that was exactly what he had been doing for months.

He had been casual when he had suggested the three blows rule to his parents the night before. They had just shrugged and agreed. After all, it was no big deal to them. It meant everything to Juan though.

Now, the moment had arrived. The children formed a queue in front of the piñata. First Antonio, at 15 the biggest of his brothers, and really a little too old to join in. He wasn't much taller than Juan though. It gave Juan some satisfaction to know that, by the time he reached his brother's age, he would be much taller than him.

Their father placed the blindfold firmly around Antonio's eyes. On the first strike, he swung wildly and missed. With the second blow, he struck the body, and everyone cheered! The third blow again made contact, but it was a glancing blow which merely caused it to spin around.

Next came Jose. He was 14, and good at baseball. Juan considered him to be the biggest risk, and he was not wrong. With his first blow, Juan stuck the Piñata hard. It shuddered. The crowd cheered. At first, Juan thought the Piñata might give, and his heart felt like it had stopped. It didn't though. The second blow again brought a big crack to its head, and it looked like one of its ears had been torn away from its body in the process.

Fortunately for Juan, Jose missed on the last swing. Juan released the breath he had sucked in. Now, finally, it was his turn.

Mrs. Perez thought she could see it in the bushes, watching, but she wasn't sure. It really couldn't be. It was impossible wasn't it?

She stared again. Now she could see it very clearly indeed. And there was no mistaking it. What looked like a very large wolf! It couldn't be? She took a photo with her camera just to make sure. As her eldest son struck the Piñata, it became agitated, and snarled. There was something wrong with it …it wasn't a wolf. It looked strange. It had so many teeth. It looked like a monster…

"Can you see what I am seeing?" Said Mr. Garcia, who was stood next to her. Is that a wolf or something in the bushes there or are my eyes deceiving me?" like her, he had taken a picture. Mr. Garcia, who was Camila's Dad, had volunteered to help out today. She didn't really need the help, but she understood that he was a single Dad and that this party was social contact for him.

"I don't know what it is," she replied, "but I think we need to get the children together, NOW!"

Juan stepped up and allowed his Dad to put the blindfold on him.

He focused. Now was the time. If he was going to be a true Jedi, and win the hand of Princess Theresa, it was now or never.

He waited. He heard the creek in the rope. Now. Crack! He heard cheers! The Piñata had been hit. Of course, as he couldn't see, he didn't know whether he had made contact with the delicate right leg. In his head though, he visualized it as having been achieved.

"Second try" said his Dad, and Juan struck again. Again, there were cheers! Juan listened for news of ultimate success, but as the crowd went quiet again, he knew it hadn't yet been breached.

Here we go, he thought. This is it. Imagine it bursting open, imagine the cheers of the crowd. Most of all imagine the victory kiss he could steal off Theresa. He swung the bat, and felt the impact. It was the perfect shot! He felt the Piñata rip! He heard the cheers! Now was his moment!

Mrs. Perez watched in horror as the creature ran. It ran across the grass straight towards her precious boys, gathering speed. It looked like a giant wolf! Except it was on two legs! She felt herself scream and she began running. Not away, as all the children apart from Juan, who was blindfolded, had, but towards her boys. She was barely conscious of the fact that Mr. Garcia, was also moving and shouting.

She was nowhere near the Piñata and her boys before the creature snatched it, pulling it from the rope, and stuffing it under its arm.

Then, in three curious leaps it was gone, off into the woods, leaving a trail of candy in its wake, like a bad figure from a fairytale.

Juan pulled the blindfold from his eyes. He didn't do it in time to see the Dogman creature, but he did see all the children, including his beloved Theresa, running away screaming. He heard the stories later though, many times from both his parents and brothers. He went on to hate the creature for destroying his ultimate moment of triumph.

It was only a few minutes later, when two black limousines pulled up. By then, the children had been gathered up. Mr. Garcia and Mr. Perez approached them. The rear window of the first car rolled down. And a man and a woman were seated in it. Both wore business suits.

"Are you hear to track that thing?" Said Mr. Garcia.

"Well yes," said the woman. "What did you see?"

"It looked like some sort of Werewolf, "Said Mr. Garcia." It was the craziest thing I ever saw!"

"We had a report that there was an escaped wolf from a private collection, the woman said, "we are investigating that."

"That wasn't a wolf!" Said Mr. Garcia.

"Does anyone have any pictures of it?" Asked the man.

"Yes, yes, I have it on my phone here." Mr. Garcia handed his phone to the man. Without speaking, the man promptly swiped it across a black laptop. Then he immediately handed it back to Mr. Garcia.

Mr. Garcia looked incredulous! "It has gone blank! What have you done to my phone you bastard! You are going to pay for it! I am a U.S vet! Tell me which damn agency you work for."

"We work for the government is all you need to know" said the man, "and if you persist in the story of the werewolf, we are going to have to make things difficult for you. You have no evidence, and you will just look crazy."

With that, the window to the limousine went up, leaving an open-mouthed Mr. Garcia in its wake as it drove off, in tandem with the other Limousine, which had also started moving. Within it, Mr. Saunders immediately turned on the sonic device. In the distance he heard dogs barking. So, he knew it was working just fine.

"This is getting harder and harder to control, Mr.McGee," he said.

"Yes you are right. We will have to ask HIM. We will have to do a deal." Said Mr.McGee.

"Who should we send though? We need a team."

"I have a good idea who the subjects might be. I am sure we can persuade them, we just need to mention the right incentives." replied Mr.Saunders.

"We will have to contact her first though. To get her prepared and ready."

"Yes, I agree" Mr. McGee Gee. "Let's do that now."

Mrs. Perez waited until she had seen both vehicles completely disappear from her view before she pulled the phone from her bra....

"I have to go back," Said Jake. I don't want to, but I have to."

"Are you sure?" Said Philip. "With that crazy jackass Rick, again? Really?"

"No, not with him. Of course not! Did you see what he pulled today?" Said Jake.

"No, I don't think I did," replied Philip.

"He had his annual conference starting today," replied Jake, "and, in front of hundreds of his acolytes, he started talking about all the things we agreed that we would not discuss! All of them!"

With that, he handed Philip his phone. It was ready to play a segment form the local news in Oregon. Philip pushed the button. On it, he could see Rick, with a black bandana wrapped around his head. He was waving and clapping to cheers "Yes, yes my people! The people of the forest are good! They want only to love us! You have all seen how they can heal us!" Their energy is the purest it could be. The Guardians are there to protect us too. Mike, Ian and I understand that. Unfortunately, the two other men with us, Jake and Simon, did not. They let fear and anger conquer them. We are better than that though. Are we not brethren?"

The crowd rose to their feet and cheered, shouting his name! "Rick Rick! Rick!" The clip ended with a commentary from a female news reporter, but Philip didn't bother listening to that. Instead, he handed the phone back to Jake.

"I thought you had all agreed NOT to talk about this for now." said Philip.

"That's precisely what we did agree!" Exclaimed Jake. "This bastard doesn't care about that though. He has gone and blurted out his nonsense of a story! Those things tried to KILL us Philip! They are not guardians at all! Since, he made this speech at his conference, I have had three journalists, including this woman here, asking for an interview. This is mushrooming."

"Are you going to take Simon again?" asked Philip.

'No not this time. It isn't going to be a good move for him. You know how he hasn't been well since this thing happened. Flashbacks. Difficulty sleeping. Problems in his marriage. Heck, I spoke to him an hour ago, and he said his wife was going mad about it all. I am not going to put him through it again."

"Who are you going to take then?" Asked Philip.

"Well, I was hoping you would come," said Jake ,"plus a few military men I know .It's going to take at least three night down there. If you can make it?"

"Count me in," said Philip. "What is your objective?"

"Whatever those things are up to," said Jake, "they are not benevolent, and they are not healing people for anything other than I malevolent purpose, I am sure of that. I mean to extinguish the threat."

The park was full. It was a hot day. The outdoor pool was also brimming with children. Their splashing and hollering filled the air, as oblivious parents sat around, having conversations about their prodigies latest achievements. It was just another summer's day. Nothing really unusual about it at all. The climbing apparatus was getting too hot to clamber on, so at this stage in the afternoon, the pool was at capacity. In anticipation of a big crowd, the city had put two lifeguards on instead of the one. Both eighteen, both on a break from College, and both looking harassed over their minimum wage vacation job, which they both thought would be easy, but was in fact proving to be anything but.

Both of them had their backs turned when it came. It moved so silently it managed to get almost to the edge of the playground before anyone reacted. The first child to scream was stood by the swings. She had one of those piercing little girl screams that resonate in your eardrums for just one second, before she was engulfed by it .It had a clear direction, but as she was just slightly off its path, it chose to divert and absorb her, especially as she resonated so much fear.

Now it moved to the pool. So many prey were there, rendered slow and easy to catch by the water they were in. It tore in a line straight through the pool, engulfing as many children as it could. The children in the shallow end were absorbed before they could even react, those in the middle of the pool had time to try and swim for the edges, but most of them didn't make it. One child would have recorded a personal best in the breaststroke had anyone been monitoring it, and this undoubtedly saved him, as he was able to haul himself out of the pool and roll away just before it got to him. One of the lifeguards, in either a moment of bravery or folly, depending on your point of view, launched himself directly at *The Black Square*, fists out. He wasn't absorbed though, *The Black Square* didn't want him, and so, he just bounced off the sides. It only wanted some of the children you see. Just like it only wanted certain adults. Some, it passed over without a scratch. Some were absorbed, but it was very careful which it chose.

There were hundreds of children in the park and the pool. It would have taken ten of them, but it only managed five before it had to leave. It was getting stronger all the time, but it still had its limits. For now.

As it started to fade, it allowed itself to linger for just a few seconds. Enjoying the screams of those it had left behind. Savoring their anguish. Then it disappeared…

Jake knew exactly who he wanted on his team. Mark Peters, a fifty two year old former infantry Sargent in the Rangers, was a good friend of his, and was very enthusiastic about going. Life hadn't been that exciting since he left the service, and this provided the perfect opportunity for a bizarre adventure. Importantly, he also volunteered to bring an array of weapons with him. "I will issue everyone with a glock, and I will also bring a pump action shotgun with me, in case we need to do any close up damage," he had told Jake on the phone.

'Very good," Jake had replied. I want to rendezvous at the Dutch Brother's Coffee stall at 2pm on Thursday. We can stay at `*The Circle*` until the Sunday morning. What I want to do is recreate as much as possible, what Rick does. I want to see if we can get the same results, however bizarre his rituals are. I also want to look for these caves where he says they live, and find their lair if possible. If it comes to a confrontation, which I don't want, then we need to be ready."

"Roger that," said Mark. "We will be good to go on all those points. In addition, I will have two pairs of night vision goggles. We can deploy those and see them coming."

"Excellent," replied Jake.

"If those things come, we are going to need them."

Paul Collins would also be joining the team. Paul was a much quieter man than the outgoing Mark. He was a former military, former CIA and had served time in Beirut, as well as a number of other Middle Eastern hot spots. He was also going to be bringing his trusty hunting rifle, which he affectionately named Betty. "I have been married and divorced four times now, and she is the only woman that truly understands me," explained Paul.

"Ha ha!" Chuckled Jake, "please feel free to bring her along then."

The last person to join them would be his friend Karl Chance. Karl loved anything to do with Bigfoot, and took any opportunity to be out in the woods.

"I think this has to be the strangest story I have ever heard," he said, "and from a friend too, which makes it all the more bizarre, but I am certainly looking forward to going. I don't have the military skill that Mark and Paul possess, but I can handle myself in a fight, if necessary."

"That's all that I need," said Jake. "That and a level head."

"I have that," said Karl.

"Then you have exactly what we need, "replied Jake.

Jake and Philip picked up a hire car from Portland Airport, and drove to meet the others as arranged. Mark had swung by Karl's place to pick him up, as he was only about an hour away from `The Circle`. Paul had driven up from Northern California, and spent the night sleeping in a Walmart parking lot, before he arrived in Bend just before lunch. Everyone was on time.

Over Coffee, Jake outlined the plan. "I have spoken to you all at length about what happened to Simon and I, at `The Circle`, last time. I don't know what those creatures were that attacked us, but I do know that they were malevolent. Whatever it is they wanted, I think we were lucky to survive. I dread to think what would have happened if they had got to us and attacked us. At the very least, we may have been taken to whatever place was that I saw through the portal, and it wasn't pretty, let me tell you. It looked like a place of decay. Rotten." Jake looked away for a moment, wistful in his thoughts of what might have been. Then he carried on. "Although we cannot be clear of their objectives, what we do know is that these creatures are NOT what he says they are. I don't know what they really want, but it is not to help or heal us in any way. Of that I am certain."

"Agreed," said Mark.

"Of course, Rick doesn't know we are coming. Not that he could stop us anyway, as it is private land. Whatever he might say, his non-disclosure agreements are worthless. As you know, he also broke his promise with us not to talk about the events that happened in `The Circle` when he talked about them to hundreds of people at his conference and to any journalist he can find who is willing to listen. I do think he is being influenced by them in some way, manipulated though. If he finds out we are here, then he may seek a confrontation."

"If he does that, then he will have made a serious mistake," said Paul.

"Yes, I agree," said Jake, but I get the feeling that he wouldn't even be able to help himself. He is being controlled in some way. I don't know exactly how or why, but I feel it is all I can say."

"He is a damn idiot, who hurt our friend," said Philip. "Simon may never truly recover from the experience he had there."

"Yes, I know how terrible it has been for him, I really do," said Jake. "That's why it is an imperative that we neutralize this threat right now. I think sleep is tied in with this, but I am not exactly sure how. I am not going to be sleeping at all when it is dark, when these things are at their most dangerous. I will try and get some sleep during the day. Mark has got enough cots for us all to lie down on. It's very important that we sleep in shifts. I can't emphasize this enough guys, I don't want there to be any point when we are all asleep at the same time, even during the day. There must always be two people awake at any one time, agreed?"

Jake paused to give them all time to consent. They all responded positively to the suggestion, so he went on, "for the first night, I want to set up the same protocols that Rick uses and see what happens. Consider it like I am trying to recreate the experiment. That means no fire, no alcohol, and putting out `gifting bowls` in exactly the same places that he put them out, with exactly the same amounts of food, in exactly the same concentrations as he had. Even to the degree of playing the same terrible music. After that, I want to change things up, and go looking for those caves, the following day, and try other things which I will brief you on as I go, but for now, that's the first night sorted."

"I think you should really rethink that no alcohol rule, and as for the music! You have got to be kidding!" Said Philip jokingly.

"I know you are joking about the alcohol Philip, but you do raise a serious issue. With all the serious and potentially terrifying stuff going on here, we can't have any alcohol drunk at all, I think. We also have all those weapons, and I don't want anybody's judgement further clouded when we have loaded weapons in our hands. If those creatures do turn up, then we are going to have to be extremely clear headed to neutralize them."

After that, Jake turned specifically to Mark and Paul. "Guys, I would like you to treat this `adventure`, if that is the right word for it in exactly the same way as you would treat a mission, as bizarre as that may seem."

"I am one hundred per cent on board with that," said Mark.

"Me too," replied Paul.

"Karl, I need to remind you that although Rick claims it was Bigfoot's that are up there, one of his followers actually told me he saw a Dogman there, and that he felt a tremendous pain in his leg before he fell to sleep. I know your passion, but I have to warn you again, that I think the probability of any of us seeing a Bigfoot is really very low indeed."

"I understand, "said Karl. "I accept that this is going to be a very tough few days. I knew it from the start when I signed up for this. I don't know what is up there, but I too am down for it one hundred percent, just like the other guys."

"Very good," said Jake "let's get the last of the supplies then, and then get up there."

'Hey," said Philip in a jocular manner," you didn't ask me how I was feeling and whether I was ready to get up there!"

"You can just do as you are told," Jake jokingly replied.

"I am good with that while we are there, but afterwards I want to hit the bar hard!" Said Philip.

"We can all hit the bar hard!" Replied Jake.

This proclamation was greeted with firm assents from the rest of the team. Philip and Jake left the hire car in the town. They could not take it up to `The Circle`, as its paintwork would undoubtedly get scratched by the journey up, with all the overhanging branches.

Jake joined Mark in his truck with Paul, as it was large enough to comfortable fit the three of them in, while Philip went with Karl in his smaller truck. Mark had already brought most of the food with him and volunteered to cook. The others readily agreed to this. They all knew from experience that he as excellent at it.

So, all that remained to get in town was as much caffeine and water as they could carry. After loading up with plenty of that, they all set off for `*The Circle*`.

Jake visibly winced each time he heard a scraping noise on the doors of the truck. The high-pitched sound sounded like screeching. Mark understandably cursed all the way up to `*The Circle*`. Jake also found himself to be very anxious on the way there too. Although not as badly affected as Simon was by what had happened, he still bore mental scars of their horrific experience. And he knew he would do so for the rest of his life...

After they got there, Jake jumped out of the vehicle first, to follow the pre-arranged plan.

He then got the others into a line, with him in the center, and rang a hand bell.

Then he raised his voice and loudly and said: "We are here to learn the truth about you, and we ask that you join us tonight. We all give our word to do no harm to you, unless you do harm to us."

"Do you think that will work?" Said Karl. "I have to say I would be amazed if it does."

"No, I really don't, "replied Jake, "but my objective tonight is to recreate the experiment as much as possible. We don't have Ian's machine, but other than that, we are good to go."

"What was the machine?" said Paul.

"Well, they all said that it was a device that opened a gateway to the other world in which these creatures reside. If that was truly the case, it would be mankind's greatest invention, right up there with fire and the wheel, I think. In reality, it was a harmless looking thing that any 10 year old might construct. Made of copper wire, a few batteries, and wood. It is ridiculous to even suggest it could do anything."

"Why do they even believe it?" asked Karl.

"I don't know for sure, and it's a good question, but I can only speculate," replied Jake. "I think with Rick, it's all about ego. He loves the idea of being special, a chosen one, a messiah with power and wisdom. With the others, they both have a deep level of unhappiness in their lives, and he is helping give them some comfort for that. It really evolving quickly into a cult, and we need to stop it, if we can. I truly believe that it's dangerous."

"The big question I have is what the creatures actually want?" Said Philip.

"I mean why go to all this trouble? Why create this whole façade?"

"That's the ultimate question really," said Jake. I don't understand it at all. It's very very strange."

"Well, lets' hope we can find out in the next few days," said Mark.

"In the meantime, gentlemen, here are your weapons."

He handed everyone a glock.

"I am good with just Betsy, I think," said Paul, unwrapping his beloved hunting rifle as he spoke.

"As you wish," said Paul, shrugging his shoulders as he did so.

"Right', said Jake, "it's important we get set up now. Mark, let's have you come with Philip and I, as we set up the gifting bowls, you can scan the perimeter as we do so."

"Roger that," said Mark.

They placed the bowls down with the exact amount of Cheetos, jam and donuts in them that Rick had also used on the first night. Then, they retreated.

The forest around `The Circle`, was silent. There was no movement anywhere.

"It's very very quiet, have you noticed," said Philip.

"Yes," replied Jake "I was just thinking the same thing."

On returning to camp, they found that Karl and Paul had been busy, setting out all the remaining equipment and cots. After that, Mark rustled up some burgers, before they were ready for the night.

"I want to try as much as possible to recreate what Rick and his team normally do when they are out here. Mark, I want you to take the 12 O'clock position that Rick goes to. Paul, please can you take the three and Karl the nine. Those are normally operated by Ian and Mike respectively." Said Jake.

"I want you to see if you can see anything that they claimed to have seen. Philip and I will move between the three places at random, in the hope of verifying anything that you may see."

They all agreed to the plan, so Jake went on, "we can switch it around a bit to stop you all from getting bored."

"Good plan, said Mark." "I will wear one pair of the night vision goggles, and you can have the other pair, for the extra nigh time visibility."

"Good stuff." Said Jake. "With that, let the music begin!"

"Oh no!" said Philip Jokingly.

'I am the worst DJ ever," said Karl, as he pressed play, and the `lift music` began.

They all took up their positions, ready for the evening. Not long after it began, Mark heard clear movement near the 12 o'clock position, but could see nothing. A similar thing happened at both the three o'clock and the nine o'clock positions. There were no belly crawling females, no playful young Bigfoots. Or the imperious elder. Nothing.

Just movement and sounds.

After about three hours, Jake called time on the activity and the music, in exactly the same way Rick would have done.

"I am beat, do you mind if I take the first shift of sleep?" said Mark.

"Not at all, you guys get some rest, said Jake. I am not going to sleep during the night. I will grab some at dawn." Philip and Paul joined him, which left Jake and Karl talking.

"I think I am going to do the same thing as you, just not sleep at night, leave it all to the day," said Karl.

"Good," replied Jake. It will be interesting to see if sleeping during the day, as opposed to sleeping at night will have any effect." Karl nodded at this, and Jake went on. "There is huge significance and emphasis put on Rick by going to sleep here. I think that's when something comes, what they are waiting for. I am not going to go to sleep and let them take me or do whatever they were planning to do to us, but we can do the rest of Rick's activities."

"Well, it's interesting that we heard movement, but we certainly didn't see any Bigfoots." Said Karl.

"Yes, absolutely," Said Jake.

The two men spent the rest of the night in casual conversation, while they listened for sounds. There were very few of those though, and dawn came as a welcome boost as it signified a little sleep for both of them.

After breakfast, they went to check the `Gifting Bowls`. The exact amount of food had been taken from them, as had been taken when Jake was with Rick and his team.

"Tonight, I want to try something different. I want to see if we can try and find out exactly what is taking things from these bowls. I would like to set some trail cams up facing them, and behind them, and some more in the forest around here, and around the perimeter of `The Circle`.

"You mean at the point where those horrible little creatures appeared?" Said Mark.

"Yes exactly, "replied Jake, "but also at other points as well."

"I have brought some marker flags. I intend to stick them in the ground at ten feet intervals on the path where the creatures appeared. If they do appear, it will give us some range as they move towards us. Help us with the targeting, and aid Betsy," said Paul.

"Well, Betsy and all our other weapons may well be needed tomorrow night," replied Jake. "Especially if those things do come. So I agree, that's very useful indeed."

"I also want to do something very important today, guys, I want to look for the caves, where Rick alleges that the Bigfoots sleep. I don't think that they really are Bigfoots of any kind, but I am not prepared to discount anything at the moment. And seeing as that may be dangerous, what I am going to do is get some sleep for a few hours before we do go, so I am relatively fresh."

"I will do the same thing," said Karl.

"Okay then, while you guys are resting, we will set the equipment up then. You can check it all after you wake up. Then we will go into town and get some coffees, to wake you up before we go to the caves. Does that work for you?" said Mark.

'It sounds perfect," replied Jake.

With seemingly non -threatening daylight now here, Jake had begun to feel very sleepy.

He lay down, and didn't wake up, until Paul handed him a very welcome coffee four hours later.

"Are you ready to do this?" said Paul.

"Absolutely" said Jake, as he began strapping on the glock.

They approached the location where Rick said the caves were supposed to be, very cautiously. Moving as softly as they could. As they approached the hillside, Mark took up the center where they might try to rush out if they attacked, along with Jake, and Philip. Karl took up the rear, in case something tried to creep up from behind and attack them.

While Paul held back with his rifle Betsy, picking an angle of elevation directly opposite to the area, ready to give precise covering fire should they need it.

"Here we go!" Said Jake. Now, he Mark and Philip circled around the hillside, ready.

"Remember guys, only shoot if we have no other choice." said Jake. He could feel his heart pounding as he turned.

There was nothing though! No cave!

"There isn't so much as a rabbit hole here," said Mark.

"That damn Rick with his constant and endless bullshit."

"It certainly seems that way," said Jake. We need to be really thorough though. And scan every part of these woods, just to make sure."

With that, the team spent all of the rest of the day, covering the forest in the vicinity of `The Circle `. In particular, they were looking for the alleged caves, but any anomalous feature would do. By early evening, they had found nothing, and so they retired for dinner and prepared to get ready for the night.

"Well if anything, not finding any caves tells me one really important thing for sure," said Philip. "What's that?" Asked Jake. "That Rick is wrong about the Bigfoots, and whatever claims he makes should be treated with extreme caution."

"I could have told you that before you came out here." Said Jake jokingly."

It's good to have the proof for myself; it makes me feel better, said Philip."

"I know, I understand, "said Jake, "let's see what happens tonight now".

When night came they took up their positions at twelve, three and nine o'clock respectively. And they waited.

"I can see something!" Said Mark, almost immediately. " There is something there!" Like a Bigfoot! A massive one! In the bushes."

Jake and Philip immediately ran over, excited. Jake peered into the bushes, but to his obvious disappointment, he could see nothing.

"There's nothing there, I am afraid, Mark," said Jake. "Yeah, I can't see anything either," said Philip.

'Really?" Mark seemed astonished "I can see it as clear as a bell!"

"What is it doing, describe it to me, and tell me what it looks like," said Jake.

"It's just stood there," said Mike. "Not really doing anything. It looks like your classic Bigfoot. Hairy, human like face, slightly conical head, like a cross between a gorilla and a man."

"Keep your eyes on it," said Jake. "If it does anything at all, then shout to us." I am going to check on the others."

"Agreed," said Mark.

Next, they went over to where Karl was. "Can you see anything?" Asked Jake. "Not a thing man." Karl replied, "I can hear movement, but I can't see anything. Can you?" He asked.

"Nothing at all." Said Jake

"I can see something, "said Philip, "it looks like juveniles, playing, this time. Only occasionally though. Like I am catching a glimpse of them, and then they are gone."

'That's interesting, "said Jake, who paused as he absorbed this. Let's try Paul now."

"Paul, what do you see?" They asked.

"I see her! Can't you? The female Bigfoot, crawling on its belly! It is amazing!"

"Again, I can see nothing." Said Jake. "Philip, what do you see?"

"I can see an outline. I can see something. A leg, maybe occasionally an arm. They come in and out of focus though. It's strange."

"I think I am seeing a pattern here." Said Jake.

"Guys, I would like you all to come together please. I have a theory about what is happening here. First, I would like you to swap places though, and again, tell me what you see."

They agreed, and moved to their new positions. "I see some juveniles playing!' Shouted Mark. "I see a female Bigfoot crawling on her belly!" said Paul.

"And just like the last time, I see nothing," said Karl.

'Philip, please can you go to each place and tell me what you see, now? "Said Jake.

"Okay sure," said Philip.

He went to each position in turn, commenting as he did so, "I can see part of the large male, I see some arms of the juveniles, I see the head of the female, and I can make out that she is crawling, but that's about it."

"What does that tell you," said Karl? "After all, I can see nothing, and neither can you."

"I think I know where you are going with this. It's about sleep, isn't it?" Said Paul.

"Yes! Exactly!" Replied Jake. "Karl and I did not sleep at all during the night. You guys all did .Rick went on and on about the importance of sleep. Something happens to us when we sleep !That's what it is They can't get to us physically right now, although I am sure they can with Rick as they are ALL asleep. What they can do though, is enter our subconscious! They can manipulate our minds!"

"That doesn't explain me, though" said Philip "why can I see stuff but not as clearly as they can?"

"I not sure, but I have a theory about that too." Replied Jake. "Tell me, Paul and Mark, how much actual sleep did you get last night?"

"I got about six or seven hours," said Mark.

"I got about the same," said Paul by way of confirmation.

"And I bet you had a restless night, Philip? 'Said Jake.

'Yes, you are right!'' Replied Philip. "I can't have got more than a few hours."

"So that's it! That's what happened then! Declared Jake. "The effects are weaker on you, because you had less sleep."

"That all makes perfect sense to me," said Paul.

"How do you think they manipulate our minds?"Asked Paul.

"I couldn't really tell you for sure," replied Jake. "We actually may never have answers to that."

"We need to be on our guard then," said Paul. "None of us should go to sleep tonight."

"Absolutely, "said Jake. "We can all sleep during the day, after we have had breakfast."

Again, when dawn broke, Jake sighed. Thank goodness, he thought to himself. Just one more night. I can do this.

They all rested on their cots that day. Nobody moved until later in the afternoon, when Jake roused himself and the others to check on the trail cams, and to check the gifting bowls.

Just as they had been on the second night with Rick, the bowls were empty when they collected them.

As for the trail cams, nothing was on any of them, except for one. When Jake went through it, he could see a deer walk up to the bowls and consume everything in them, before leaving.

"That shows that wild animals take the food, then," Said Paul.

"Yes, I think it does," replied Jake. "It doesn't do that on the first night though. I would guess that something that they control, takes it on the first night, in specific quantities. It keeps the interest level up, make it look like there is something here showing intellect, not just random animals. After that, it allows passing animals to eat it."

"This whole place then is an illusion." Said Paul. "It's designed to deceive people!"

"Yes." Said Jake. "I am sure that some of the `healings` happen, but ultimately they are not for a benevolent purpose. I don't know what that purpose is, but I just know it isn't a good one right now. And Rick is no prophet."

"Bring on the night." Said Mark. "I am ready."

As darkness enveloped `*The Circle*`, they began taking up their respective positions.

They were all on high alert. Jake and Philip stayed in the center, ready to respond.

The first thing they did was to go to Karl's station. "Again, I see nothing." He said.

"Me neither, "said Jake. "How about you, Philip?"

"Well I can see something, but not very well", he replied, "It is more like a silhouette now."

"Good," that would indicate that the effect of whatever mind manipulation they have done to you, is starting to wear off. Like their technology, their control has its limits," said Jake.

'I am very relieved about that," said Philip.

"How about you guys," Jake shouted across to Paul and Mark. "I can see the big one still, but it is fading, not as clear," said Mark.

"Same here, said Paul. "It is like I am looking at ghosts rather than tangibles."

Jake put on the night vison goggles to see if he could get a better view of any potential subjects with them. Mark already had his on. It was then that he saw it. Red. Pulsing through the forest, something. A shape. Amorphous. It did have a purpose though; it was slowly coming towards them.

Mark, I can see something red at two o'clock, can you see it! "Yes I can, and it's impossible!"

"Why is it impossible?" Asked Philip.

"Because you can't see red through these cameras! Yet we can!"

"Get ready to open fire!" Shouted Mark.

He was ready now, with his shotgun.

"I am worried it is a distraction, I will cover our rear, just in case," said Paul.

That was the last thing he said, before the Dogman punched straight through his chest as though it were butter, and withdrew just as surgically. The mistake it made however, was to enjoy the agony on Paul's face, as that gave time for the others to open fire. It reeled as it absorbed the shots, and then flew straight back, as Mark began firing the shotgun into it. It did not get up.

"It's physical, we can win!" cried Jake defiantly, trying to get everyone to focus on that, rather than the horror of what had just happened. Then suddenly the red mist formed on the track, and began to open up. As it cleared, Jake started to see through it. There were those horrible little creatures with the piercing red eyes, but this time there were many more. In an instant, he now realized that they faced overwhelming odds. He immediately shined his light straight at the portal. In response, it stuttered, but did not close.

"They are coming! Quick, use your lights!" He shouted.

*The Black Square* went straight into the back of Mark. It squeezed as it did so, liquidating his vital organs. It irritated it to kill like this; its favorite thing was to enjoy the suffering on its victim's faces. However, his masters wanted it to be quick. They only wanted one of the humans not to be killed. So, it did as it was told, as it knew that if it didn't, then the consequences would be pain.

Now the remaining men saw *The Black Square* coming towards them. It confused them, and they were horrified to see Mark so swiftly dispatched by it.

"No!" "Shouted Jake as it turned and headed towards Karl, "quick, help me to shine your lights, stay focused! Our only chance is to shut it down now!"

Fortunately, both Karl and Philip responded and turned their lights towards the portal, as *The Black Square* bore down on them.

The instant they did so, it disappeared. Along with the body of the dogman, and *The Black Square.*

Only the two bodies of Paul and Mark remained.

The horrified survivors stood together panting. They waited to see if there would be another attack, but none came.

When daylight finally came, Jake slumped to the ground.

Barbara Ellis just felt wonderful. The pain was gone, everything was normal. They had just been to see the Doctor and he had confirmed the news. The cancer was gone! The Doctor had called it a miracle. And indeed it was. It was a miracle that Rick had bestowed upon her. As she sat next to her proud and smiling husband, she had never felt so happy. Apart from when she had first got married. She did not regret that decision. And she knew that she was doing the right thing to leave most of their money to Rick. After all, he was helping people. Helping them get stronger. So, she had changed her will. Eighty percent of her and her husband's will would now go to Rick, with the remaining twenty percent to the dog charity. They had no children, and with nearly eight million dollars, Rick would be able to do a lot of good for people. He just lacked resources, that's all. In the future, he would have plenty of money. And two million dollars would still have plenty of homeless dogs, she reasoned.

She had driven this highway between the Doctor's and their house so many times over the last twelve months, that she barely even noticed it. She looked at her husband and smiled. They were going to have a happy future together. She felt so good. Thus, she barely noticed when something seemed to take control of the wheel. She had no time to scream, no time to react as it drove her and her husband into the tree. The coroner would say that `they probably didn't feel a thing` when they died due to the swiftness and intensity of the impact. In fact, they had, well Barbara had anyway, but not for long. Then she was dead.

Larry and Pete always loved fishing at the weekend. They especially loved this particular lake. Pete was also an excellent cook and there was nothing, I mean anything in the world better than catching a fish, and then cooking and eating it that very same evening. As fresh as fresh could be. It didn't really need anything added to it.

Today, Larry was in one of the two kayaks they had brought, while Pete stayed behind on the shore and fished there. Pete waved to his friend, in response to his wave, which demonstrated he had just made a mighty fine catch. It hadn't been the best of days for fishing, previously he had managed to get two smaller fish, and Larry had got nothing, hence his decision to go out on the kayak.

It felt stronger now. Stronger than ever before. Not just stronger than these humans. They were nothing to it. A disease. Or a sport. It was just able to stay here, in this world, for longer than ever before. It didn't de- materialize. There was no pain. All it had to do was kill. Kill in a special way, just as the masters had ordered. They wanted it to generate fear with its kills. And so did it. So, it was easy enough to accomplish. There was another thing too. There was more of its own kind. For a long time it had thought it might be on its own. A thing that existed only in the shadows. In and out of time. Sometimes existing, sometimes not. It had seen two others now though. It knew that one of those was dead, but the masters had promised more to come soon. And it believed them. It had been hundreds of years since it had hunted in a pack, but it no knew that time was coming again soon. Oh, how sweet that would be! How amazing! For now though, he would have some sport with this other one, destroying the humans. If anything, it was even more vicious than it was, which was could, as it made it more emboldened.

Pete wasn't really sure if he had seen it. It didn't really look real. Like a wolf maybe, but much bigger. Was it a dead dog or something, floating in the water? Surely not?

Larry was now making for sure, with their dinner, so he didn't see it.

Now, Pete could see that it was in fact swimming. Swimming towards Larry's kayak! He shouted 'Larry Larry! Look behind you! WOLF!"

He could see that at first Larry was straining to hear him. Then he seemed to laugh, thinking that Pete was joking. He still decided to look behind him though, and whatever he saw, caused him to paddle harder than he ever had before, in fact furiously.

Pete wished he had the gun, but he had left his revolver back at the cabin. It was only eight hundred yards away, but with his bad leg, he knew he would never make it there and back in time to help his friend. All he could do was shout and encourage.

The thing that was swimming at Pete could easily have got him by now. It had moved so rapidly on the first few seconds, that he was sure it would engulf Pete almost instantly. Yet now it hung back. What's it waiting for? Larry thought to himself. Maybe it has thought better of the encounter and decided not to pursue him. Not least as it had seen and heard him shouting as it began the pursuit.

Larry was getting nearer to shore now. The creature in the water, whatever it was, did not seem to be coming any nearer. Pete began to relax. And started to think about dinner. Then, suddenly it came rushing out of the water, hurling itself towards Larry. Pete could see that he was exhausted by now and couldn't move any faster. Indeed, if anything Larry seemed to be going slower, his energy spent.

Then, the creature grasped the stern of the kayak, and twisted it, which led to Pete being submerged in the water.

Larry could see splashing briefly, but that was it. He waited anxiously. He shouted, but there was no response. He began taking off his shoes and socks in readiness to swim over. He knew he might not be able to save his friend, and he was certainly afraid of the creature in the water, but he was damn well going to try.

The kayak overturned then. Pete was still in it, only this time he didn't have his head.

The creature held it up; looking straight at him, in the same way that Pete had held the fish up. It was a horrific sight, made all the more so by the fact that it seemed to be trying to send him a message. Was it mocking him?

Pete turned in response to movement in the periphery of his vision. There was another one of those things now. Twenty feet from him. Just staring. It was on two legs, and grinning through a part opened mouth, with twisted and seemingly incongruous teeth.

In that instant, Pete knew that he had to make it to the cabin where the revolver was. He doubted he would, but he knew it was his only hope. So, he would do his best.

He began limping towards the cabin, as fast as his leg could drag him. It was painful. By now, the creature that had killed his friend had emerged out of the water, and the two of them began walking slowly towards him as he staggered the short distance to the cabin, dragging his leg agonizingly as he did so.

They could have killed him easily of course, but they didn't they waited. He knew why now. They were hunting him, and toying with him as prey! Like a cat hunts a mouse.

As he reached the door of the cabin, they began to run at him, like they had been waiting for this precise moment. He knew exactly where the revolver was. He knew he would die, but he was going to hurt those damn things first. He flew through the door and slammed it shut. The revolver was on the kitchen table, with a box of bullets by its side. He concentrated to load six into it as rapidly as he could, even as he heard the banging against the door. He was able to fire two shots off, as the other creature burst through the window, and skewered him, one of which made impact into to the beast's shoulder.

The creature watched the human writhing as it died. Enough pain with this one, but not enough fear. That lack of fear had slowed its movements, and now it was hurt. This wasn't a satisfying reward at all. Either for it, or its masters. It would have to kill again soon…

# Chapter Seven

# Into The Fairy Kingdom

The moment Rick saw it, he knew it was perfect. This compound was exactly what they were looking for, it would be ideal for their needs. Indeed, THEY had told him to buy it. First, they had come to him in dreams, but now they had been able to form themselves occasionally into orbs. Orbs of glowing light. Almost spectral in their quality, except Rick knew that this was no ghost. It was creatures trapped into another world, and he would help them. In return, they would help him. He had always known he was special, destined for greatness. Other people could be useful from time to time, he granted them that. Now though, he was really becoming what he needed to be.

A prophet. A leader. A chosen man.

He had called this press conference at the lovely new ranch he had bought with Barbara's money. It was a shame she had died so soon after being healed. That's sometimes the way things go though in life, and ultimately by helping him, she had served a greater purpose. That was a wonderful legacy for her, he reasoned to himself.

They had also wanted him to call the conference. They said it was time to raise awareness. In just three short months, his followers had gone from double digits, to thousands. Building work on the 20-acre complex had already begun, to ensure everything would be ready. The special healing church was a particular focus, and the construction teams were on double time here. They had also wanted that. And Rick was only too happy to oblige at this stage, he would do anything they wanted. With the donation in Barbara's will, he would now never have to work again. He was particularly glad about that, as he didn't like working all that much, and despite the fact that he was intelligent, he changed jobs frequently out of boredom, and because he found that people always underestimated his true abilities. He could also live here, with his followers.

They only really had one requirement. That he bring people here to this place to be healed. They didn't ask for anything else. AND they were doing good, so how could he refuse? Of course, he never asked for any money himself either. If someone was to give a donation though, then he wouldn't refuse. That was obviously the will of God, wasn't it? They had never said that they were from God, but they must have some connection with him. If they weren't though, a part of Rick who considered this as a possibility, really didn't want to know.

They had encouraged him to call this press conference, and he was excited. His reach was widening. As well as the local press, there was now national and even international news following his movements. He could actually see a crew from the BBC here! His followers, all proudly portraying new purple T-shirts with his face on them, had arranged the chairs, and brought up the twelve sick children who stood before them. Or rather, nine of them still stood. Three were too sick, even to stand for a few minutes, and so they were in wheelchairs.

Rick walked up to the podium to thunderous applause. Waving the crowd down with smiles, he waited for silence. Then he spoke:

"Ladies and gentlemen. We are now presented with a unique opportunity. A unique opportunity to do good! I am here to tell you that. All they have ever cared about, is helping us. Some of you in the audience today have borne witness to that. Have seen miracles be performed."

Rick paused to absorb the cheers and applause from the crowd, and then he went on: "Last week, as you know a terrible tragedy occurred. Two men were killed by their own friend's it seems, at the very spot where we and they have done such good. A place of healing became a place of murder. Yet, although we weep for those men who died, we must not let their loss destroy what we have built. No! Ladies and gentlemen, for that would be letting the defilers win!

Fortunately, we still have the opportunity to heal. For those who do that, have agreed to come here, to this compound. Which we have called the Barbara Ellis Ranch, in honor of her generous donation.

We now have, as you can see, twelve children before you. These children have all been examined by independent Doctors. Sadly, tragically, they have all been found to be terminally ill. Tonight, they and their parents, plus any medical Doctors they wish to have with them, will spend the night at our ranch. All of them have been given medical permission to be here. THEY will come in the night. They will heal them. We have been blessed. Tomorrow you can come back and judge for yourselves."

With that, Rick finished speaking and left the podium.

There was uproar from the crowd and the press, and then Ian addressed them. "Ladies and gentlemen, ladies and gentlemen! Please! We made it very clear that there would be no questions today. The children are tired and we must proceed with letting them rest. You can all come back tomorrow morning, as we agreed, and then Rick will take questions."

Rick walked off the stage and downed his glass of iced juice. He knew that this was the biggest night of his life. If they delivered, and he pulled it off, then he would be everything he had always wanted to be, an international celebrity. If he didn't, then he would be forever stigmatized as yet another charlatan. He knew what that was what the press, apart from the by now friendly local press, wanted to categorize him as. He expected their cynicism .Which is exactly why there would be no press until the following morning. Then he would show them …

Kyra and Kevin Reed had been childhood sweethearts. Everyone had called them the perfect couple. Even their names had blended together. When they had married, at her Mum and Dad's traditional little white and wooden Pentecostal Church in Tennessee, he had been so happy. Kevin knew that all he would ever want in the world from then on was her. Forever.

They had had two beautiful children together, their little angels. Perfect, a boy and a girl. The boy had dark hair like him, and the girl had curly blond hair, just like his lovely wife. They had both been good children, they had never really given them any problems. Some people said that that was because they were excellent parents. Kevin knew that that wasn't the case really though. They were just intrinsically good people. Heck, even with them both into their twenties, he and Kyra still called them their `little angels`, now.

He would have stayed liked that for the rest of his day's and lived his life perfectly happily. Then, unfortunately, things changed. Bill came along you see, and with Bill his marriage was destroyed.

He hadn't really meant to look at her email. He never read her texts on her phone, even when she left it lying around. He considered it a matter of principle. She may have occasionally looked at his. He didn't know, and quite frankly he wouldn't have cared. He didn't have anything to hide. She had left her email up on the computer you see. Recently, he had got into gardening. He was finding that he really enjoyed it now. He got pleasure from nurturing plants, watching them develop. He liked his garden neat and tidy. Just like everything else in life. His desk was neat, his car was immaculate, and he even enjoyed tidying up after his wife. So, that Saturday afternoon, he had decided to go on the computer in order to look up what new potted plants he would like to buy for their increasingly beautiful garden.

Kyra had left her email open. He was about to just close it down though, when he saw a mail unopened from Bill. It caught his attention because it's title was `What I Would Like To Do To You `. Kevin opened it, and to his horror read what Bill proposed. It was quite clear that Kyra had been doing all sorts of unspeakable things with Bill. Things he had never tried with her or would never even dream of trying.

In that moment, Kevin felt his world destroyed. Of course, he had confronted Kyra with it, and to his surprise, she hadn't denied it. When he questioned her, she seemed almost relieved, like a pressure inside her had ended. Since then, he had read a lot about affairs. Kyra's explanation for it was very common. She had been bored, wanted a bit of excitement, and Bill, who she worked in the same office as, had provided it. Kevin had to concede that since he had confronted her, she had been very remorseful. They had been to marriage guidance counselling. He had listened as his faults were discussed with a third party. A woman he had never met before, who asked him lots of irritating open questions. He had answered politely. In truth though, he had hated it. He hated the woman. He hated the situation. He hated his life. He had just kept up the pretense. They had started making love again a month ago. It just didn't feel the same though. Before the affair, it had felt like they were two people intertwined, just one being. Now he felt like he was banging a ten-dollar hooker. He was actually surprised he still got an erection.

He had to concede that since her terrible betrayal, Kyra had done her best to repair the relationship. She had immediately ended it with Bill. She had even changed jobs. It was her that had arranged the marriage guidance counselling. He was polite for now. You wouldn't know it, but underneath all he did was hate. He hated her for what she had done to him. At first, he thought he might forgive her, and that his hate might abate. It didn't though. He knew now it was never going to, and that he could never forgive her for what she had done to him.

When she had suggested this long weekend in the Olympic Forest in Washington State with the kids, he had had agreed. Despite the smiles and his seemingly happy demeanor, he knew that this would be the last time they would ever spend any time as a family together. Although the rest of them didn't know it, he had planned to move out a week after they got home. He already had his place. He was enduring the long weekend for the sake of the kids, not for the sake of Kyra.

Russ was the first to spot it. In the middle of nowhere, stood a giant wooden staircase, ornately carved. Then, they had all circled around it, but there was nothing around any of its sides. It seemed to lead to nowhere.

"I am going to go up it," said Russ, Kevin's son. "No wait!" said Kelly, you shouldn't! I have read about these things! People are saying that they are appearing and that when people go up them they are disappearing!"

"Nonsense "! Said Russ laughing. "With that, he bounded up the stairs, and stood straight on the top. "See, nothing at all!" He laughed triumphantly.

'Let me try", said Kevin. "Be careful honey," said Kyra, but of course Kevin made no comment to this. He had read the stories of people disappearing from the staircase too. He also wondered if any might be true. He though it unlikely though. Unlike his son, he climbed the stairs ponderously, carefully. When he got to the top, he closed his eyes and wished himself somewhere else, anywhere else but this place. He heard his wife's screams, but they now seemed so far away, yet he knew she was nearby. When he opened them again, he realized that he had made a big mistake. For wherever he now was, Kevin instantly realized that he was in a terrible place...

They had decided to tell the truth. Jake, Carl and Philip had all agreed it was the only way. Mark and and Paul were definitely dead, and there was just no point lying. They could have said it was a bear, and they certainly did discuss that, but at the end of the day, they all knew that wasn't the truth. Jake had wanted to stop this area being used by Rick, and to destroy the creatures. That had been his objective. After Karl had called the Police, and with their imminent arrival, he felt that he had at least achieved that end. The place would become a murder scene. He hadn't stopped the creatures, but maybe they needed `The Circle` for some reason to cross over from their world, and without it they could not. He certainly hoped so. In the meantime, as well as mourning the death of his two friends, he also had to consider the fact that he stood a high chance of being charged with murder, or some other serious crime associated with it. No Judge was going to believe that a Werewolf and a killer huge black square, or whatever it was had killed his friends at the behest of those creatures from the other side of the portal.

It was clear that the Police who first came up to investigate did not. After their transport to the station, they were immediately separated and arrested. There they waited.

The following day, Jake was bundled into a police van. He could tell that what had happened had attracted some media attention, as he heard reporters outside shouting questions, and what sounded like cameras flashing. Now he realized that he was becoming some kind of celebrity over this, but in the worst possible way. In the best case scenario, Rick and his friends in the media would now portray him as some kind of criminal, and he would certainly lose his job, if he hadn't lost it already by now. In the worst case, he would be going to prison for murder. Either way, it didn't look good.

Karen Pearson was bored. So bored. At first, the astonishment at what had happened to her had kept her going. The fact that this world was so similar and yet so much the same was fascinating to her, and amusing. At first, she had thought she might be having a psychotic breakdown. That would explain her mysterious and unexplained absence from work of course. However, it didn't explain all the other differences, even the relationship ones. Her mother was also different. In this world, she was just that bit colder. Probably because here, her father had been dead three years. Whereas in her own world, he was still a vigorous member of his local tennis club. She had resigned herself to her fate though. She couldn't see a way back. So, she had tried to get on with things as best she could. They hadn't allowed that to happen though. So, she had been detained, against her will, for `psychiatric evaluation`. And what a nebulous term that was. She was tired of stodgy food and disingenuous conversation. So, she just decided to not cooperate anymore. And then, a few days ago, she was moved here. Wherever `here` was. She had been given a room and her own clothes back, even allowed to wander in a small but pretty garden at the back of the building . She felt that things were shifting. For what purpose though?

There was a knock on the door, and then, without waiting for a reply, two men immediately entered her room. Both were wearing grey suits. Must be some kind of uniform for this world, she thought.

"May we come in?" Asked one of the men politely.

"You already are in," replied Karen in a surly manner. She had had enough of shrinks.

"Allow me to introduce us. I am Mr. Saunders, and this is Mr. McGee."

"Are you here to give me another diagnosis?" Said Karen.

"I am really not at all interested you see. I know what I am and where I am from. I could fake it and tell you what you want to hear. That I had a breakdown. That I feel remorse that I have caused my friends and family to suffer. In truth though, I don't want to do that, so I am not going to. You see, Mr. Saunders, I hate it here. I hate your bland food. And my family sucks. Even your TV. Is terrible. I can't actually believe you have something called `Celebrity Love Island ` as one of your most popular shows. Your world is ridiculous. So, drug me up and fatten me up if you want to. I just don't care. I am ready to switch off."

"Actually Karen, I believe you," said Mr. Saunders, who was smiling as he did so, "and so does Mr. McGee." At this, Mr. McGee nodded, to reinforce his agreement.

"Is this some reverse psychology thingy?" Asked Karen, suspiciously.

"No, not at all. We really mean it. We believe you. I fact, we **know** you are from a parallel world. And we have learnt all we can from you, so we are going to try to get you back. It will be expensive to keep you here, a place you have no desire to be in. So, it's best for all of us."

"Get me back? How though?"

"Let me take you to meet some people, we can all talk together, I think that's best."

Jake sat in what looked like a briefing room. He noticed that it was really hot in the room, as though somebody had broken the air conditioning, but when he went to look for the air conditioner control, he couldn't find it. So, he sat there and waited. Feeling increasingly and uncomfortably hot.

Eventually though, some people walked into the room. He was glad the door was opened, just so he could have some relief from the heat.

Two men and a woman entered the room.

"Karen, this is Jake, Jake this is Karen," said Mr. Saunders. Jake, "I am Mr. Saunders, and this is Mr. McGee."

"Pleased to meet you all "said Jake politely. I am going to get two more of our experts into the room, to save time, and then we are going to conduct the briefing. With that, he pressed a button on the desk he was sat beside. A sliding door on the other side of the room opened, and two more women entered the room. They nodded to Jake and Karen, and then sat opposite them.

Jake and Karen, this is Tamara Reid, who is a physicist at Harvard, and Camilla Evans, who is a psychic medium. They all exchanged introductions, and then Mr. Saunders went on.

"Mr. McGee and I work for a division of the government. It doesn't matter what division that is, suffice to say that we do. And we want to help you. Both of you face bleak futures. You Karen are stuck in a world that you don't belong in, and don't want to be in. You Jake are facing a murder charge. With this, they both looked at each other warily.

"Don't worry, you will have plenty of time over dinner to tell one another your stories. Indeed, it is an imperative that you must. For now though, we want to give you both information, so just listen if you will please. Tamara, can you start," said Mr. Saunders.

"As you know, my name is Tamara Reid, and I am a physicist. Recently, a brilliant young friend of mine was murdered in broad daylight by something that we did not know existed until it killed her. A horrible interdimensional creature we have just nicknamed *The Black Square.* We do not know where it is from. We do know that it enjoys killing particularly children.

With that, Tamara pressed another button in the console, and a projector came on. "Now, watch this footage." On the screen, Jake saw a child's party, with a piñata. Then, suddenly a giant werewolf like creature ran across it, stealing it!

'And finally, before I tie it all together, this. She played the footage of Rick's press conference. Jake could not help himself and let out an audible groan at the sight of one of the creatures that had murdered his friends.

"We have known about what they call the `Dogmen` for some time." Said Mr. Saunders. We also worked out long ago, that as they have no evolutionary pedigree, they must be interdimensional creatures. There were few of them, and their attacks on humans were so very infrequent, that we could contain the stories about them, and have them dismissed. This was in order to stop people panicking of course. Now though, they are getting bolder and killing people more often. In broad daylight too. *The Black Square* is new to us. If anything though, it's even worse. We think that they have been brought in by those creatures you saw, that have formed a connection to Rick. And they are accelerating the process. Even trapping people using staircases linked to their world. Despite our best efforts, we are no longer able to contain it. We need to stop them.

"Why though, to what purpose? Asked Jake.

"Yes and why are these things killing so often? Asked Karen.

"Well, said Tamara, "we think we have worked out the answer to that. Simply put, those things, *The Black Square*, the dogmen, even those creatures you fought Jake, are feeding. Feeding on fear. In their dimension, thought has real power, it is able to manifest actual physical objects. And through his vanity and ego, they made a connection with him. His friend Ian built a machine, which is ostensibly useless in our world, but they have replicated their own. Using them together, they are able to make a connection between the worlds. Think of it as thought manifesting reality. Of course, it's more complicate than that, but I don't want to confuse you."

"Thanks for the vote of confidence," said Karen.

Then Mr. Saunders interjected and said: "suffice to say that we have to destroy both machines, otherwise these things could start to come through in large numbers to seek our energy. And it would be horrific, have no doubt about it."

"How can we stop them, and why do you need us?" said Jake.

"I will explain," said Mr. Saunders. "Karen here is from a parallel world. Very similar to ours, but there are some subtle differences. Her double is probably enjoying her life right now, while she is here. You have seen these creatures that are doing this. Simply put, they attacked you when you busted their plan. Both of you believe in seemingly impossible things. We need you to go into their world and destroy that machine that is in it. We can take care of the one in this world."

"Why us though, and why should I do it? Or her?" Said Jake.

"Well, as a starting point, neither of you have anything to lose. She is stuck in a world she does not want to be in, and you are facing a murder charge. We can get you off that of course. And your friends too. You have to help us though. So, allow me to let out second expert take the floor. Camilla, if you please".

Camilla Peterson smiled and then spoke. Unlike Tamara's more clipped tones, hers was liquid, and lilting. Possibly an Alabaman, Jake thought.

"Jake and Karen," she began, "as Mr. Saunders said, I am a psychic. I want to elaborate on what that means. You are both, I take it, familiar with mediums, people who have the ability to speak to the dead?"

"Yes". They both replied. "Well, I have that ability. I also have another gift too. I can speak to what we like to call `The Good Folk`. You would know them as Fairies."

"Oh come on!" Said Jake. "I don't mean to be rude Camilla, but are you really serious?"

"Hear her out, Jake." Said Mr. Saunders.

"Jake, since I was a girl I have been able to see dead people. At first, it greatly disturbed me, as you might imagine it would. As an older child, it brought me comfort. Of course, my parents were very worried about me. They thought I may be a schizophrenic. I had lots of treatments to make me better. I spent a lot of time at home. Especially in the garden that was where the fairies spoke to me. They are a real people Jake, they just exist in dimensions beyond ours. They do communicate with us, but they are erratic and capricious. Think of them as brilliant, vain and fickle. Especially their King.

You have seen remarkable things Jake, you now know other worlds exist. It cannot be too much of a leap for you therefore, to now accept that creatures your ancestors have written about for thousands of years do actually exist."

"I am certainly down with it," said Karen, "I am after all, from another world, the only difference is I look just like you, and they, I would imagine, look a little different."

"Exactly," said Camilla.

Jake shrugged. Then he said: "I have to concede that I have seen strange things I never even thought remotely possible before .I did wonder why I scientist and a psychic were on the same team. It makes sense now though."

"We select the best people from whatever the discipline," said Mr. Saunders.

"Only a few decades ago, the motion of parallel universes would have been seen as scientific heresy in many quarters," said Tamara, but now with the expansion of our knowledge of inter dimensional and quantum physics, we are much more open to consider these seemingly bizarre possibilities," said Tamara.

"Why us though? Said Jake, "and how are we going to get the fairies to help us?"

"That's an excellent question!" Said Mr. Saunders.

"Of course, we have known about the fairies for many years now. That they were real. We knew that they abducted the occasional child. We don't think it is for a truly nefarious purpose, but we are not sure why they do it. Yet, it was so infrequent and erratic we could never get a pattern to trace them. They are clever, it is difficult to predict their moves. We have tried to communicate with them, but they always refuse all contact. Occasionally they will accept gifts off Camilla, and exchange pleasantries, but that is all. We think now though, that they might respond to contact.
"Why now?" Said Jake.

Those creatures that attacked you are interdimensional. They are using technology to do it though, whereas for the fairies it is instinctual. It is part of their nature. These things are interfering with their world as much as ours . If they destroy us, they destroy them. The analogy I could draw is rather like polluting a beautiful mountain stream.

Your mission is simple . We want you to go in and destroy their machine The one that just looks like the one we have here, in our world."

"And, we also want you to bring some samples of their world back," added Tamara.

"Samples?" Said Jake.

"Yes samples. A few rocks. Dirt. Organic matter if possible. We feel that analyzing this information could help us stop them in the future," replied Tamara.

"And how are we going to find the machine?" Said Jake.

"You are going to ask the Fairies for help." Said Mr. Saunders. "I think they will know how to find it. And how to travel into the realm of the creatures who built it."

"Well, this sounds like a lot of fun," said Karen. "It also sounds extremely dangerous to me. What do we get out of it?"

"You get an opportunity to get home. We do not have the technology to get you back yet. We are working on it, but it may be decades away. Help them and they will help you. For Jake, we can get him and his friends off the murder charge. If you don't go, then you will stay here, hating it forever. If he doesn't go, Jake faces a different but just as bleak, future.

You are perfect for this mission because you do believe in what seems impossible. Unless you have the gift that Camilla possesses, which is so very rare, in order to make a connection with the Fairies, you first have to believe in them. That is impossible for our soldiers to do, sincerely. Yet for you two, having had the experiences that you have had, it is much much easier."

"I am down for it, I have nothing to lose," said Jake.

"You leave at dawn," said Saunders. "We have learnt that the fairies never operate in the dark. They particularly like mornings, it seems, and it is already 7pm now. I should warn you though, that things are getting worse. This happened today."

Saunders pressed on the button on the console in front of him, and Jake and the others watched as Rick addressed a press conference. Rick was on the podium. In front of a very animated crowd, Jake frowned as Rick started to speak.

"Now you have seen the power of what has happened ladies and gentlemen! Now you know what they are truly capable of! The Doctors have confirmed that all these children have just been HEALED! It is a miracle! What we can accomplish now is almost beyond words! What good we can do!"

With this, the crowd in from of Rick roared their approval.

Mr. Saunders pushed the button again.

"We think they are somehow accelerating the process. Using this vain idiot to help them. Somehow, the energy generated by children particularly help them. Most especially if they are sick. They thrive on two energies. Fear and disease. If they do find a permanent way into our world, rather than a temporary one, they will no doubt spread both."

"Let's do it then." Said Jake.

"Don't worry my love," said Camilla," I will get you there."

This race had been exceptionally hard, but it was nearly won. Thirteen miles, across exceptionally difficult terrain, and he Brad, was on it. He was only 800 yards from the finish line. A year of effort was about to pay off. With his confidence growing now, he ventured a quick look behind him. There was nobody. The crowd could see him now, and they started to cheer his name. He relished it! Yes, he thought! My time has come!

Indeed, it had come, but not in the way he had imagined and hoped for. One second he was on his own, the next two giant wolf men were running on either side of him, matching his stride. At first, both he and some of the crowd let out a little laugh, thinking it might be some kind of prank, or people in costumes joining him for the last few yards of the run. Then though, Brad noticed something about the `suits` as he turned to his right. The teeth had saliva on them, and the eyes blinked! This was no suit! The moment he stopped and started shouting, was the moment the Dogmen reacted. They each grabbed one of Brad's arms, and shot off into the woods. Hundreds of people saw them do this, but they didn't care, in fact, the Masters encouraged them to behave like this. It wasn't like before, when they had had to sneak about in the shadows.

They carried him for many miles between them, enjoying his adrenaline and terror. He was such a sweet kill, they wanted to drain every last drop of fear out of him. And he did so much writhing and kicking. Eventually though, they had to kill Brad. You see after all of that effort, they were hungry.

"I know that I have seen some incredible things recently, but this still seems a little weird," said Jake.

"Belief is really important Jake," said Camilla. "Our enemies use it as a weapon. You must focus now."

"Yeah Jakey boy, the human race needs us now. Who would've thought that, "said Karen. " Camilla, can I have a drink, you know like a whisky or something, before we do this?"

"It is 7 am Karen. You can have one when you get back. A double." Camilla replied.

"Or two." Said Jake.

They had arrived at the garden. Karen and Jake listened while Camilla gave them instructions. Jake noticed that Mr. Saunders and Mr. McGee as well as Tamara the scientist had now deliberately stood back as she did so. All three were watching intently.

"I am going to ask them to join us now," said Camilla. "Two very important things you must know though. Firstly, if they do show up, try to keep composed. No sudden movements. And secondly, if you are taken to see their King, whatever you do, do not eat or drink anything he offers you in the Fairy Kingdom."

"Why not?" said Jake. "If you do, he will claim you and you will stay there forever. They have different values to us. They are not intrinsically bad, but they are tricksters, that is their nature."

"It's gonna be hard if they offer me a spicy chocolate cake," said Karen.

"Spicy chocolate cake? Really? Your Universe is weird, "said Jake.

"I am serious," said Camilla. "Eat or drink NOTHING."

"Okay," they both replied.

With that, Camilla began singing, and occasionally twirling. She seemed to be almost in a trance. Jake suppressed laughter, he thought would be inappropriate. The situation was ridiculous, really. Yet his cynicism quickly turned to astonishment. Firstly, Jake watched as a little green door materialized in the tree they were standing next to. Then two figures emerged. One was a little man with a red hat on. And a white beard. The other was a beautiful little red headed fairy, in what looked like a shimmering silver dress.

The Gnome, for that was what he must be, Jake reasoned, had a big frown on his face, and his arms folded. He seemed cross.

'What is it, Camilla? "He said.

"These two seek an audience with your King."

"Why?" Replied the Gnome. Seemingly even crosser than he had been before". He is very busy. Why should he bother himself with the affairs of humans?"

"We have a way to defeat the dark one's. I know they are your enemies too. These humans, Jake and Karen, would like an audience with him to speak with him about that."

Jake saw that Bumble turned to the beautiful fairy who gently said to him "yes, he would want it". With those words of reassurance, Bumble then seemed to relax.

Immediately, two tiny pieces of cake appeared on a silver platter. She held them up to Jake and Karen.

"You can eat them, but nothing after that," said Camilla.

"You are going to shrink shortly. Down to their size. Don't be alarmed. It should only be temporary."

"Should?" Said Karen. She took the cake anyway though.

"Good luck!" Said Mr. Saunders. "And don't forget the samples," said Tamara.

As she was speaking, Jake watched as he literally shrunk before Camilla's legs. It was a strange sensation, like being pulled backwards on a rollercoaster. When the process stopped, he found himself to be tiny, albeit slightly the tallest of the group although he could now not have been more than fifteen inches tall.

Jake looked at the fairy, open mouthed. She was even more beautiful close up, he thought. She had soft features, and beautiful green eyes. She had just the tiniest scar on her cheek.

"Stop drooling at the Fairy, Jake, "said Karen, "because if this is a double date, I am not doing it with the Gnome."

"Ha ha ha!" Laughed the Fairy in response to this.

"My name is Charlotte, and this is Bumble," said Charlotte.

"I am Jake and this is Karen," replied Jake. She smiled at them both, but Bumble still looked stern.

"We will take you to meet our King. He won't have long with you, so be concise."

"We must go through the door over here, which Bumble will open for us, as he is a gatekeeper."

"And stay on the path," Bumble added, a little sternly.

"Too trippy," said Karen. "If I had known this existed I would never have bothered buying weed".

Jake felt his heart pounding as he went through the door. Beyond it, a beautiful meadow stretched out. It was a wildflower meadow, and the colors were so vivid that Jake almost had to look away from them, because they gave out their own luminescence. He also could see people sat in the midst of them, and now, when he focused, he could also hear some whispering.

He turned to Charlotte, and asked, "can I hear something? What is it?"

"Ah," she replied. "It's the flowers. They are already talking to you. In one way, it's a good sign. It means you are well connected to nature. Now though, it will make it easier for our King to read your mind as a result."

"I understand," said Jake, and thank you for the advice. She smiled back at him.

Jake glanced at Karen. She winked at him, and he looked away, embarrassed.

Then she said. "Hey Bumble, this is a pretty place you have here. Such beautiful flowers. What are all these people doing though, randomly sat about. They all seem to be sat on their own. Are you guys into picnics for one, or what?"

Bumble replied. "They are humans, not fairies. They have been called by the flowers. They stay there now, amongst them. That is why you must stay on the path. Some have been there for centuries, as you would say. Time is different here. It takes us a lot of effort to focus on it as a linear concept in the way you do."

"Sheesh, I won't be going near the flowers then, damn right!" Replied Karen.

After an hour or so, they came to a small village. At the end of it, Jake could see that there was a Castle, medieval in design, with huge white turrets.

"I take it that's the King's place then?" Said Jake.

"Yes," said Charlotte, "We are nearly there."

The village itself was exceptionally quaint. Lots of lovely Tudor style cottages with neat little well tendered gardens. Almost everyone seemed to have a fountain as well, Jake thought. The place was very quiet though. As they passed through it, the silence was peppered with only the occasional bird tweet.

"Where are all the other Gomes and Fairies then Bumble?" Said Karen.

"They smelt you coming, so they have left until you have gone." replied Bumble.
"Our noses are much more sensitive than yours."

"Smelt us coming? Really! I am so not staying in this Universe, said Karen, "the chances of me getting laid are like, zero."

Coming to the end of the village, they passed over a moat and a drawbridge. The Castle's entrance was guarded by two huge troll looking creatures in armor. Each one sported an enormous two headed axe. Neither of them said anything as they approached. They both stood motionless. Like statues. Indeed, Jake thought they might be just that, but as he passed by them, he saw one of them blinking.

Charlotte led the party, to a huge marble covered hallway. At the end of it was a huge wooden door. It looked very thick, but when she knocked on it, her movements generated a surprisingly loud sound, Jake thought, almost as if it were hollow.

"Your Majesty" said Charlotte. "It is Bumble and Charlotte to see you. "And we have brought some visitors. Humans. They would seek an audience with you."

"Yes yes, Charlotte. I saw you coming in the scrying mirror. You may bring them in," replied the voice through the door. Although it was high pitched and very quick, Jake could tell that it belonged to a male.

With that, Bumble opened the door and they all entered the room. Jake immediately thought that it looked like a medieval banqueting hall. There was a huge dining room table in front of them. On it was crammed a gargantuan amount of food. Food of every kind. Just with a quick glance, Jack could see chickens next to chocolate. Ice cream next to beef. All the dishes looked exquisite . Yet there was no order to them. They were all set out in a very haphazard manner, it seemed.

There were two huge fireplaces to the left and right of the dining table, on which flames danced amidst a multitude of logs. What really drew Jake's attention though was the figures at the far end of the table, which he reckoned, must have been about thirty feet long.

Two little girls sat on either side of the table, and they were eating, one with blonde hair, and one with dark. There was also another fairly, unlike Charlotte though, this one had long slivery yellow colored hair. She however, wore a gold dress as opposed to Charlotte's silver one. She was drinking from a goblet, which she had just poured from a pewter jug as they walked in. The most striking figure of all was in the main huge chair at the opposite end of the table. He was very thin, with a shock of brown hair. On his head, he wore a plain gold Crown. He was immaculately dressed in crushed blue velvet, which looked Jacobean by design. He too, was drinking from a goblet. He watched them for a second, his eyes flicking between them as he did so. Then he smiled, before slowly putting down the goblet and addressing them.

"Ah welcome to our Kingdom! This is so very unusual! You must have had a long walk!" Said the King.

'Your Majesty. This is Jake and Karen. They are humans. From parallel worlds. One is from the world that we interact with."

'Thank you Charlotte! Bumble, stop looking so cross! I know you don't care for human adults all that much, but really, these are our guests."

"Please! Jake! Karen! Take a seat! Help yourselves to some food and drink! Anything you want ", said the King.

"Err, I don't think so Mr. King, "replied Karen "We were specifically told not to eat or drink anything while you we were here."

At this, the King again smiled. "You can't help me for asking though, can you? It's my nature." This time though, as he asked his next question, he spoke much more directly and deliberately slowly.

"What is it then that you want?"

"We want you to help us battle the creatures from that evil world that seems intent on destroying us all," said Jake. "They are using a machine to move between the Universes. Unlike you though, they are doing a lot of damage. They are bringing in other terrible creatures. We will take care of the destruction of the machine in our world. We want you to help us get to their world. We don't know how."

"Do you like us Good Folk, Jake?" Said The King, in response.

'I don't understand the question," said Jake. "I have never come across you before. I like Charlotte and Bumble."

"Yes," we can all see you like Charlotte," laughed the King. Here, in our world, one's passions are easy to read, aren't they Charlotte?"

Charlotte said nothing in response to this, she just blushed and turned her eyes down, shyly.

"You have read about us as a child. Never really considered us as anything other than fantasy. Until yesterday. Mr. Saunders and Mr. McGee will no doubt have given you a briefing on us. Most of what they say is true. We are an entirely different type of species to you. We have always been, though fortunately, unlike your kind, there are not that many of us. We live for many hundreds of your years, and we have very few children. Indeed, every fairy child is celebrated by all our community. They are so rare. Travelling between worlds is easy for us.

We abhor technology. As you perceive our world, it has no sophisticated machines. We choose that you see us like this, in this medieval age. It is the period of your existence which we liked the best. As your dependence on technology increases, I am afraid that our world's will sadly become farther and farther apart.

Those creatures that you described. We know them. We call them the Vilal. Think of them as like an intelligent Virus. They have destroyed their world, and its resources, and they must now take from others. Their technology is superior to yours, but not by that much, maybe a generation or two. Soon, you would catch up, and they know that, so they had to act fast. They do share some similarities with us. Thought is an energy Jake, all emotion is, and it can be used. If you only knew how, thought could power all your machines on Earth. Emotion is also energy. The Vilal, and those other creatures which are their minions, feed off energy. Whereas we feed off love and kindness and purity, they feed off fear and anger. Sickness and death. They are essentially evil." Then he added, "look around the table Jake. Look at the two little girls. Are you familiar with them?"

"No, I don't think so," replied Jake.

"Isabella, would you stand up for me please my darling?" Said the King.

At his command, the little girl immediately rose to her feet. "This Jake is your sister, Isabella. You see her now as she is and also as she was when she disappeared."

Jake was stunned "Isabella, is that really you?" he asked.

"Yes, it really is," said Isabella. "Jake! You have grown so big! I am sorry that I am still the way I am .I have fun here though, all the fairies are so gentle and kind."

Jake then turned to the King, his anger visibly mounting.

"Now wait Jake! Said the King. "There is an important difference between us and the Vilal. In your culture, there are stories of Fairies abducting children for centuries. We do it very rarely, and only with specific children, in very specific circumstances. They have to be very intelligent, and have a good imagination, so they can see us. We have also chosen to take just the terminally ill. If she had stayed in your world Jake, your sister would have been dead of leukemia within six months."

At this, Jake looked around the room, both confused and shocked by what he had heard. His poor parents. If they had known she was still alive, he thought.

"'Now I know you don't trust me, Jake, and I understand why. I rather think you will believe Charlotte though for some reason, eh? Said the King. "Charlotte, am I telling the truth?"

"He really is," said Charlotte. "Everything he says is true, Jake".

"Can I take her back with me?" Asked Jake.

"I am afraid not. She will have to remain here, said the King. "Although she was not diagnosed with cancer by your Doctor's at the time of her abduction, she would have been within a matter of months. And she would have been dead not long after that. We saved her sweet and pure energy here, and now this is where she belongs."

"What about those other things, the Vilal you called them. What do THEY want?" said Karen.

"They are the opposite of us. They feed off disease, and fear. They convert it as a resource. They have used this man Rick's fear and ego to build ever stronger bridges into your world. Soon they will have a permanent lock, and they won't need him or anyone else. At that point your people will become enslaved, and eventually your planet will become barren, just like their world."

"Won't they just build another one, that machine that Ian built wasn't really effective, it was something that a child could build frankly," said Karen.

"Ah but it isn't the capacity of the machine, it is the thought that made it so, the *thought* that manifested the connection. It isn't about the machine's intrinsic capability, it's more about what it represents, especially to its creator. Most especially now, given the unique set of circumstances in which it was built.

"Ian could easily build another one though, if he wants to," said Karen.

"Ah my dear, Ian won't ever be building anything again, I can assure you of that. Millions of lives are at stake .He will be- how do you say it? Taken care of, by your people. Look, this won't stop them forever, I know that. It will push them back though. Humans are starting to catch up on how the Universe actually works. Maybe it will buy you enough time to actually be able to match their technology when you do have to confront them. For that time is certainly coming, make no mistake about it."

"What do YOU actually want, though, your majesty", said Karen, a little sarcastically.

If the King picked up on the sarcasm, he didn't acknowledge it, for he immediately replied, "ah I want you to succeed! I want you to win!" and he clapped his hands together as he spoke.

Now he turned to Jake and said "those flashlights in your backpack won't help you Jake, nor will that revolver you have strapped to your waist. I will give you weapons." With that, he clicked his fingers, and a sword materialized in his hand. Charlotte and Karen also had one, while Bumble was given an axe.

Then, the King continued, "Charlotte and Bumble are experts with the weapons I have given them. I know you and Karen are not, but they will work, if you have to strike the creatures, they will die. And this time, it is YOU who will have the element of surprise."

"How will we know where to go though?" Asked Jake.

'Bumble will take you. He is a tracker .He will help you find the machine. It won't be far from where he opens the door. He will imagine the location of the machine before he opens the door to their world."

"And do we get anything in return?"

"Ha ha ha!" Excellent question!" Laughed the King.

"You Karen, get to go home. I can make that happen for you no problem. And as for you Jake, you can get to come here more regularly and see Isabella! You would be a hero even of our people. I might even let you marry Charlotte eventually. She was going to be my sixth wife, but alas, she has that scar on her face now, so she can't be."

"I am sure she is very disappointed," said Karen. Jake on the other hand, felt a mixture of surprise, and excitement. He said nothing, but stole a glance at Charlotte, who smiled back.

"Then we have to proceed! And quickly now, for things are moving swiftly in your world now, as they should. It means though, that the Vilal will soon be on their guard, and a surprise attack won't be possible."

Jake quickly said his goodbye's to Isabella, promising to return to see her. Then, he and Karen, together with Charlotte and Bumble, walked out of the Palace. They immediately turned left after crossing the drawbridge, into some woods. They walked through them, as they path twisted and turned, and the forest got denser and denser. Until eventually they reached a tree with a little brown door. Unlike the other door, this one had chipped brown paint on it, and a rusty handle.

Now Charlotte turned to address Jake and Karen, while Bumble closed his eyes and concentrated on the door, holding its handle and mumbling under his breath.

"When we go through the door, you will see a blue light around you. Think of it like a bubble. That is your atmosphere. You cannot breathe in their world without it, just as they cannot breathe in your world. We may see other humans there, but you must not talk to them. They will only distract you. We must get to the machine and destroy it, and leave as quickly as we can. We will soon be detected, but not immediately I don't think."

"Do you understand?"

"Agreed" said Karen.

"Yes," said Jake.

With that, Bumble opened the battered door, and they all stepped inside…

Ian was happy now. In fact, he was the happiest he had ever felt in his whole life. He had never really amounted to much, in truth. That was how he felt anyway. Now in his fifties, he had no heirs, no dependents, and both his parents were dead. When he was gone, there would be no trace of him left on earth. Nobody would have remembered him. No legacy at all. Just like a lot of humanity these days. Not anymore though. Things were going to be very different from now on. For he, Ian, had built the greatest machine ever built by mankind since the dawn of time!

It was right up there with the wheel, and fire! A machine that was used by aliens from another world! He could only imagine how many statues would ultimately be built of him. How many Universities would be named after him? He was lonely, more than anything though. Crushingly so. Maybe this business would help him get a girlfriend. It must do really, he reckoned.

He had terrible trouble sleeping at the best of times, but now even more so. So, even though the click was barely audible when his room door was opened, he still hear it , or thought he heard it. It couldn't be though, as he had licked it from the inside. So, he kept his eyes shut.

He opened them quickly, when he felt the jab in his arm. Then he saw her. A beautiful woman was stood over him, she smiled at him. He smiled back. Then she put a finger to her lips and mouthed `shh`.

With her other hand, she softly stroked his cheek. He was enjoying this, and started to become aroused, wondering what might happen. Then, he caught sight of the other figure. Ian could only make out a silhouette, but from its build it was obviously a male. And it, or rather he, was carrying the machine! At that point, Ian tried to cry out, to struggle. He realized though that he couldn't move. The woman carried on stroking his face and smiling. The last thing Ian thought before he went to sleep forever was that she had kind eyes. And such a lovely smile...

The first thing Jake noticed when he stepped into world was the light that surrounded him. He focused on it in fact, for he was somewhat reluctant at first to look around, as he was loathe to think what horrors might await him when he did so. He found that whenever he moved his arms and legs, it moved to, even when he circled with his new sword, it was always around him. This gave him some confidence. Charlotte seemed to know what he was thinking, "It is your atmosphere Jake, but unlike on Earth with the air you breathe, this one is a part of you. It won't be broken."

"Ever?" Said Karen. "Not unless you lose consciousness. Or ..." Charlotte replied.

"Yeah, I get it." Said Karen.

Now Jake looked around. The sky had a red hue to it. There was a sun, only the sun seemed far away as though it were muffled by something. As Jake began moving, he heard an audible crunch on the ground. He looked underneath his feet, there was matter of some kind, but it disintegrated as he stood on it. It felt like it had dried out a long time ago. Jake bent down to grab some of the stones that were lying around on the floor. Several of them just crumbled to the touch, but he was able to pack four or five that seemed quite sturdy. He began putting them in his backpack.

"What are you doing, Jake?" Said Karen.

"I am gathering samples for Tamara," as she asked, he replied.

"We need to get moving, it isn't far, but they will detect us soon, said Bumble."

"Yes, we have felt the energy shift somehow in your world, " said Charlotte. "I can't see what has caused is as I am here. The Vilal will know though, and that will make them more alert."

They began moving across undulating hills of barren red earth. It was very hot, and by now Jake was thirsty, but he would not have drunk water from this world even if there was some around. Trees were not uncommon. They looked desperate and twisted though. None of them had any leaves on them. They were barren, just like the rest of this world. When Jake touched them as he walked past, he felt bark just crumble off them half the time, and it subsequently turned to dust in his hand.

"Do you know what has caused this, Charlotte?" said Jake.

'We think a mixture of war and environmental pollution. They are a very arrogant and selfish species," she replied.

"Even more than humans?" Said Karen.

"Even more so." Said Charlotte. "We have felt them. They consider everything, even members of their own kind who they judge `inferior`, to be an expendable resource to use as they see fit. And their supreme arrogance has also led them to think in the short term. And ultimately contributed to the destruction of their world. Now, they seek other worlds and other resources to exploit and ultimately destroy. And unfortunately for you, they have found yours."

"Well let's stop the bastards," said Jake. And with that, they pressed on.

"There is a city or town of some kind coming up in front of us," said Bumble, "I am afraid that we cannot to around it. It would take far too long, and we would certainly be detected. After we have passed through it, we need to climb the hills behind it. On top of one of them, we should get to the place where they are keeping the machine."

From their vantage point, Jake and the others took an opportunity to rest and look down at the city. Most of the buildings seemed to be made of a kind of glass of some kind. With various colors in evidence. Many of them seemed to have suffered damage though. In the center, Jake could see an enormous green glass building, which had a huge spike on top of it. It was undoubtedly beautiful. It too was cracked though, broken and twisted just like the rest of this world thought Jake.

"Hey are those people down there?" Said Karen.

Jake squinted and he could make out human shapes, they seemed to be pulling a large piece of glass, which was supported by a wheeled platform. Possibly part of a building? Then to his horror, he caught sight of some of the Vilal. They were stood supervising. They occasionally pointed. At this distance, he could not make put what they were holding. He could see though, that intermittently they would prod the humans with it.

Charlotte came to stand by his side "you can't help them Jake," said Charlotte. They are changed forever. They have been physically manipulated to breathe this atmosphere now. Even if you could rescue them they would die almost soon as they entered your world. In any event, your people don't have the technology to alter then back."

"I understand," said Jake. "We need to stop this now though."

"And we shall, I promise," said Charlotte soothingly.

"How are we going to get through the city and remain unseen?" said Jake. Surely they will see us the moment we go down there."

"Bumble and I can create a `glamour`, said Charlotte, "think of it like a cloak of invisibility. They won't be able to see us, but it will only last for a few hours at most. How long will it take us to get through the city, and too our destination, Bumble?"

"I think we can make it, "said Bumble. "We mustn't dawdle though. Once we go in, we are committed. I doubt there will be any trees down there we can use to jump through to escape back into the Fairy Realm. I can't sense any at all. However, there are some on the hills behind the building where the machine is though, I can feel them."

"Good "said Charlotte, "now it is imperative that you listen to what I am going to say next, Jake and Karen. When we go down, we have to be totally focused. If the Vilal sense us, then we will be captured. It won't be pretty."

"I understand," said Jake. "Me too", said Karen, "I want to get home, and if going through this city of bastards is what it takes, then I am down for it."

"There is one very important fact you do need to understand before we do go down though," said Charlotte, "as you know, the Vilal live on strong negative emotions. Whatever you see, and I mean whatever, you must not interfere in what is going on down there. More importantly though, you must not try to feel negative emotions. Anger.

Hate. Anything like that. If you do, they may sense us, and we will all die."

"Deep breathing Jake, deep breathing," said Karen.

"I have got it, "said Jake. "You can trust me."

It took them less than twenty minutes to enter the outskirts of the city. Even though they were invisible to any potential assailants, they still moved very cautiously as Bumble whispered direction to them. The city seemed mostly empty. Jake caught sight of a few of the Vilal in the distance, but they were always far off. "Bumble is trying to find a route that avoids most of them," explained Charlotte. "Fortunately, they are relatively few compared to humans. A mixture of war, pollution and arrogance has seen to that."

"Good "said Jake. "If we do end up at war with these creatures, then one advantage us humans will have is superior numbers."

"Let's hope we get to the machine and destroy it to give time for your technology to catch up with theirs," said Charlotte.

All the buildings were made of glass, but very few seemed in good condition, most had panes broken at the front of them. They passed various machines as they walked through the streets. They seemed rusty and were in various states of decomposition. "Their atmosphere is toxic," explained Charlotte, machinery rusts, so that would explain why they are so big on glass here. "

"It also means that the machine Ian built will corrode quickly too, hence their sense of urgency," said Jake.

Suddenly Bumble halted. "There is no quick way round the next two sets of Vilal, they are more of them on this side of the city. If we get through this part though, we will soon be through it," he explained.

In front of them was a building, which crackled and hummed. Jake could see that Vilal were coming in and out of it.

They crossed to the opposite side of the street to avoid them, but as they passed the building, Jake took the opportunity to look through the window .Through it; he could see four Vilal, sat around what looked like a black sphere. Energy, in the form of four red beams of light were connecting them to it. They all had their mouths open, seemingly in ecstasy at the experience.

"Are those damn things getting off on that sphere or what? " said Karen.

"In a way, yes", said Charlotte. "I can sense that that sphere stores negative energy. Simply put, they are feeding."

"How horrific, "said Karen.

Bumble moved them along with a swish of his hands. "We are nearly out, see, the buildings thin out there. All we have to do is pass by the river and the building next to it. Then we can climb up the hill and reach the machine to destroy it."

Now they started to walk by the bank of the river. Jake tried not to gag as he approached it. It was bright orange, and smelt rotting, like chemicals that had turned bad. On the opposite side of the river, there was a building. Unlike the other they had seen though, this one looked like it was made of iron. Rusted iron, but iron nonetheless. It the middle of it, was what looked like a giant gear. As they got closer, Jake could see that it was being physically turned by four humans, who were walking and pushing it using handles protruding from it. It seemed to require some effort, as they were straining as they did so. To his horror, Jake could see that they were chained together at the feet, so they could barely shuffle. Two were men chained together, while the other two were a young man and a young woman.

Three Vilal were with them. Two were on the ground. They occasionally prodded the humans with what looked like a white glass rod. One more stood on a raised platform above them all. Almost like it was supervising, although Jake realized it could just as easily have been simply enjoying the suffering of the humans.

As they got to the point where they were parallel to them, Jake stopped and turned to Charlotte and said: "isn't there anything we can do for them?"

"No nothing. She replied. "Remember what I told you. They have been permanently altered to breathe in this world. Even if we were to attempt a rescue, and succeed against all the odds, they would die if they left this world."

"What are they doing?" Asked Karen, "I mean why are they doing this manual labor? Their technology, as warped as it is, is superior to ours. So why are they turning this wheel?"

"It has no particular purpose," said Charlotte. "They are not utilizing the energy from the wheel turning for anything. Rather, they are feeding off the energy of the misery it generates in the humans for having to continue with the task."

"What bastards they are!" Said Jake.

"Jake, remember keep calm," said Charlotte. "They will sense your anger."

As she spoke the Vilal on the platform slowly turned towards them.

"Calm, Jake," whispered Charlotte, "your anger is starting to allow them to sense us."

It wasn't the only one. One of the humans now peered across towards them. Jake could see that he was part of the couple, and he began saying something hurriedly to the woman he was tied to.

"We are done for," said Karen. "That couple has spotted us."

"Quick run!" Said Bumble.

It was the actions of the couple that saved them. The man, who's human name was Jamie, had told the woman by his side to scream. Had she not, and in doing so distracted the Vilal, they would all certainly have been captured.

The Vilal now turned their attention to the couple, and with all three in obvious irritation, they prodded them with the rods in their hands. Both of whom in turn, let out audible gasps of pain as a result.

"They saved us," said Jake.

"Yes" said Charlotte, "the Vilal would have captured and tortured us before we could reach the machine to destroy it. Now, let's make their sacrifice worthwhile."

Finally, they now began climbing a hill which led them out of the city.

A few minutes later, they rounded a bend, and Bumble halted.

There, in front of them was a building which looked like it was made of black obsidian. Unlike many of the others they had come across, it was unscathed.

"There are two Vilal in there with the machine." Said Bumble. "Jake and Karen, do you think you can fight if you have to?"

"Undoubtedly, "said Karen. "I am ready for these bastards, "said Jake.

"Remember, said Charlotte, "we only have to destroy the machine. Then we leave."

They entered the building. Inside, it was dark, and at first, Jake had difficulty seeing. Gradually though, his vision adjusted to see spartanly furnished rooms. There were glass bottles containing organic body parts, of goodness know what, thought Jake. A few tables were peppered here and there with what looked like tools of some kind. Other than that, there was nothing. Now, they moved as a team toward the center of the building. "It's in here," whispered Bumble. He cautiously opened the door to the room he stood in front of.

The two Vilal in the room immediately saw them, and Jake could see that they were surprised for they both stared opened mouthed at them in shock. Although that quickly turned to a sneer of disdain. Jake now felt their eyes, as red and piercing as ever boring into them. Then, one of them spoke:

"Humans and other creatures! We have to admit that we were not expecting you. Now you are here though, let me assure you that your stay will be permanent."

"I don't think so, little monster," said Karen. At this, the Vilal laughed. Jake thought to himself how deep the laugh sounded considering the size of the Vilal.

Then, it went on: "you are a pathetic and weak species. And these others are no better. Our technology is far superior to yours. We shall conquer and use you. You stand no chance at all."

As one of the Vilal addressed Jake directly, the other was moving towards a panel on the wall.

Charlotte immediately saw what it was up to, and leaped across the room, swinging her arm high above her head, she severed its arm, and it fell back shrieking. The other Vilal now launched itself at Jake swinging what looked like a short club made of a black glass. It screamed as it rushed him. Jake swerved out of its way instinctively, as he realized that it too was making for the console, just like the Vilal before it. It pushed the button, and a horn instantly sounded. Then it turned to Jake and said: "we have been especially waiting for **you**. We shall make your suffering especially painful." Then it swung at Jake again. This time, he parried its blow, and then twisting his arm, he thrust straight into the body of it. The sword pierced it cleanly and easily. Like rotten fruit, Jake thought. It died instantly.

With the alarm now increasing in intensity, both Karen and Bumble had wasted no time in smashing the machine to pieces, using their respective weapons.

"We have to get out of here! Now, quick we have to find a doorway before they all come!" Said Charlotte.

They left the building as quickly as they could. "There are trees on the nearest hill side .I think one of them would work," said Bumble.

As they climbed towards it, Jake risked a look behind him. He could see a line of hundreds of Vilal running out of the city, up the hill, towards them. In their own atmosphere, they moved very swiftly, much quicker then he and his companions, and he realized they would soon be upon them.

"Quick!' Jake shouted. They are nearly here!"

Bumble now worked the tree to produce a door. It materialized, but when he went to open it, there was nothing there.

"It won't work, it does not have enough life force left!" He said to Charlotte.

He looked frantically around. He spied a larger one, about thirty yards away, which looked very similar to an oak. "That one!" He shouted. Now though the creatures were almost on them, and as they ran towards it, Karen shouted, "we are not going to make it before they get us!"

"Yes you will!" Said Bumble. With that he stopped, and turned. He then shouted "Forever!" Defiantly. The creatures halted their pursuit just for a second, and then gleefully rushed him. As they got to him, he exploded in a cacophony of color. There was screeching, and Jake saw several black limbs fly overhead, just as he and the rest of the group reached the tree.

"Bumble! Bumble! "Shouted Charlotte.

"Charlotte! You have to open the door! Open it now Charlotte or he will have died for nothing! "Said Jake.

"Yes!" Said Charlotte. She manifested the door and opened it. They ran through, and she shut it, just as the creatures who had survived the blast rushed the final few paces to the tree. They were back in the Fairy Kingdom. They were safe.

The King was on the other side of the door already waiting.

"You did it!" He said clapping his hands in delight as he spoke.

"Congratulations!"

"Bumble did not make it, your Majesty, I am afraid to say, said Charlotte. "He died so that we might live."

'Yes, I understand". Said the King. "I felt him. As I feel all my people. He shall be known forever as a great hero amongst us, for his sacrifice."

"We are all very grateful for what Bumble did for us." Said Jake.

"I would offer you something to eat and drink, but I know you can't have it, "said the King.

"Unfortunately, I can't," say Jake, "and given the urgency of the situation before we left, we should really report in, and tell them what happened."

"Not we," said Karen. "You".

Jake turned to her, looking puzzled. "Jake that world is YOUR world. Not my world. I want to go home." She said.

"I understand, but I will be very sorry to see you go."

"Oh, I somehow think you will be okay," said Karen. She turned and winked at Charlotte as she did so, who blushed in response.

"Now, your Majesty, if you would be so good as to do the honors."

"Of course, "said the King, "it would be my pleasure."

The King effortlessly swept his arm across the nearest tree. With that, a yellow door appeared on it.
Goodbye Jake ', said Karen. "And good luck with your future. Wherever it takes you."

"Thank you, "said Jake. "Safe journey home."

"Goodbye all you wonderful wierdos!" Said Karen waving as she entered the doorway. With that, the door slammed shut, and Karen disappeared back into her own universe, never to return.

"I want you to go with Jake, Charlotte, and help him," said the King.

"Some of the nastier creatures still remain in their world, and now they are trapped there. We especially need to make sure that *The Black Square* is destroyed."

"Yes, your majesty," said Charlotte, and after she had curtsied to the king, she led Jake by the hand to the door. This time it was a red one. Smiling, she stepped through it, and Jake willingly followed.

He was now in his own world, and still small. "Just close your eyes, and imagine yourself bigger and you will be", said Charlotte, gently".

"Sure" said Jake, smiling back.

He did as instructed and then felt nauseous as he grew bigger. When he opened his eyes again, Jake was his normal size. And by his size, stood Charlotte, now just slightly smaller than him, and still holding his hand.

Camilla was waiting for them. She watched calmly as they grew.

"Welcome back, "she said. Dare I ask how you got on?"

'It was a success". Said Jake. "I am exhausted though. How long have we been gone? "

"Nearly 72 hours," said Camilla...

'It feels like less than a day to me," replied Jake. "It would explain the serious dehydration though."

"Come my dear. And you too Charlotte. Let's get you some food and drink. Of course, Mr. Saunders and Mr. McGee want to see you too."

"No doubt," said Jake. Then he turned to Charlotte and said, "Can you eat food in our world then?"

"Oh yes, she replied "and you will be able to eat in ours too, if the King changes it so you can. We need his permission. That way you won't have to stay if you don't want to. You will be able to come and go as you please."

"We should ask him then," said Jake "I would like to continue our friendship when all this is over."

"As would I." replied Charlotte.

Jake went through a battery of medical tests when he returned Charlotte was also offered the same treatment, but she refused.

Eventually, being refreshed, he was able to join Mr. Saunders and Mr. McGee for the evening briefing that they had arranged.

"Feeling better?" Said Mr. Saunders as they walked in.

"Yes, much, "Jake replied as he walked in.

"Excellent." Responded Mr. Saunders.

"And you, young lady," he said to Charlotte, "So good to see you too. You are I believe one of the Good Folk? Well do please join us."

Mr. Saunders smiled at them both and offered them seats opposite the desk where he and Mr. McGee were sitting with both Camilla and Tamara.

"I must say that your timing has been excellent," said Mr. Saunders.

"We are about to see if a couple of those samples you brought us back from the other world will actually work."

With that, Mr. Saunders dimmed the light, and they all turned to a screen facing them. On it, Jake could see a man and a woman, in what looked like a log cabin. They seemed to be just talking.

"This is our trap." Said Saunders. "We have been able to trace the Dogman's movements quite effectively using their kill patterns, and the probable distance they might be travelling. We also know their sensitivity to sound, so we have been playing that to try and channel then towards this cabin. We have also used some of the samples that you gave us. We think that they may be able to sense them, and come looking for them, as they are now no longer connected to their master's. It was Tamara's idea, and I have to admit, it was a brilliant one. We haven't had anything `bite`, so to speak for hours, and then one of our snipers on the perimeter edge thought he saw one in the shadows . They have now been confirmed by multiple snipers as moving towards the cabin."

"What about the people inside though?" Said Jake.

"Wait and see," replied Mr. Saunders.

The man and the woman inside the Cabin seemed oblivious to the imminent danger, but Jake realized that they must in fact be aware to some degree.

Now, they were both sat opposite one another at a table, seemingly chatting. The man had his back to the door, which was about six feet away from the table.

Jake watched as a huge shadow crossed the window, and then passed to the other side. The man and the woman continued their conversation.

Then, the door to the cabin burst open, and a huge dogman came smashing through it, launching itself towards the back of the man, and at the same time, Jake could see another one burst in through the window, moving purposefully towards the woman. Clearly, the creatures had been stalking their victims, and hoped to surprise them from two sides. However, the reaction from the two potential victims was just as swift. The woman raised her hands from the table and began firing a revolver straight at the head of the creature that was moving the man, calmly firing over his shoulder directly at it. For his part, the man had turned, and was now firing into the creature at the window. The two creatures both seemed stunned by the firing, and both of them reeled back from the attack. They seemed to howl, and then steady themselves. Indeed, they may have had time to recover, and still finish their potential victims off, if they had not then both been engulfed by men carrying what Jake thought, looked like machetes. It was over quickly.

"Mr. Saunders, the creatures have been dispatched," said a male voice which clearly emanated from the room. Jake could see that it came from of the black clad soldiers in the cabin, as he had now turned to directly face one of the cameras contained within it.

"Congratulations Henderson". Said Mr. Saunders. "And tell your team well done too."

"That's one down, one to go, as they say." Said Mr. Saunders.

"What do you mean?" said Jake.

"We still have to destroy *The Black Square*." Replied Mr. Saunders. "That's more dangerous than even these creatures."

"Why is that?" Asked Jake.

"We think it is very intelligent, said Mr. Saunders, "and also evil, of course."

Now he turned to Charlotte and said, "please can you tell me anything your people know about it? Anything that might give us an edge."

"It comes from another world from yours, that's true. In fact it, and the one's you call the Dogmen, are both from different worlds. The Dogmen's Universe has more links with yours, so it was easier to bring them over, and they occasionally manifest here already, as you know. The Vilal brought them here to create more energy derived specifically from fear. It helps them to manifest, to get a stronger footing in your world, so that they can come over permanently. As you know, The *Black Square* was also brought here by them, but from a different world to the Dogmen. The Good Folk fear it the most because it is so intelligent and cunning, and it also likes the energy from children. Particularly sick children. Only unlike us, it seeks to harm them."

"Why children though? Said Jake.

"There is something about their energy that you might find difficult to comprehend." Explained Mr. Saunders. "As a child, your energy is more concentrated. Less so as you get older. The Vilal wanted both *The Black Square* and Rick to bring them children. Especially sick ones. So it can harvest their energy. It used them in different ways. Rick, however misguided he is, just wants to help them. *The Black Square* however, enjoys killing them. "We have set a trap for the Black Square as well today. We shall see how that goes." Said Mr. Saunders.

"What about Rick?" Said Jake.

"Oh, we think his power will abate now that the Vilal are not helping him. Let's just say that we will keep an eye on him, just to make sure though," replied Mr. Saunders.

*The Black Square* approached the school. It thought it had smelt children. It was hungry now, really hungry, and it wanted their energy. The place was quiet though.it stopped and sensed the air. There was the *smell* of children yes. There was something from the Vilal here that was for sure. There were no other creatures though. There were only men. Men who were trying to trap it.

It saw one in a tree, hidden . Crudely, it thought. There were more of course, fanned about in different places. They had underestimated it. It moved closer to the school, and it felt two of them close in behind it. Then it struck. They had no chance to even fire their weapons before it absorbed them. It was still strong and quick, not as strong as when the Vilal had been there, but strong enough. It felt the impact of the bullets from the others as it left, but they of course, did no damage whatsoever. It would have liked to have stayed and killed more of them, but it just didn't have the time. It had to hunt for the energy it really needed, as it was starving now.

The next morning Jake felt good. He had had a wonderful rest, and Charlotte was still there, in the next room. She had promised to stay for at least the foreseeable future, so she could provide a comprehensive report to her King. Over breakfast though, his mood was to change.

"I am afraid we are going to need your help just one last time, Jake," said Mr. Saunders. "We were not able to destroy *The Black Square*. It sensed our trap. We have to destroy it, and we need you and Charlotte to help."

"How can we help?" Said Jake.

"As you know," said Mr. Saunders, "we were able to lure and destroy those two dogmen in by baiting them with a trap. We tried the same thing with *The Black Square*. It wasn't having it though. It sensed the trap. And in the process, it managed to kill two of our special forces soldiers before it left. As you know, what it really wants to do is to kill children. We are not ever going to use them as bait, of course. However, you two are the next best thing. You are from a different world, Charlotte, and Jake you have recently travelled to one. And both of you have met the Vilal. Simply put, we are going to arrange it so that you are the only targets available. That is, if you would be so kind to agree."

"I agree," said Jake, "I am ready to end this." "As am I," said Charlotte.

'Thank you" said Mr. Saunders "We can't have it running around killing children."

"So where are you going to put us?" Said Jake.

"Why in a school of course." He replied ….



*The Black Square* could see its perfect prey now. Two Children in fact, one of them really quite sick, although its parents did not know it yet. Perfect for the kill. It moved silently across the meadow to where the family was playing.

Mike Owen was getting a bit tired of summer. He wanted some fresh air, but his favorite season was fall. He wasn't keen on the heat, but his kids were restless, so he had agreed to take them out to burn off some energy, despite the bizarre news reports. He had watched the news bulletins talking about these strange things killing people, and initially he had dismissed them. Not this time though. Luckily, he had looked up before he kicked the football towards his son. As a result, he saw it. It was moving straight towards the kids. "Get in the car now!" He shouted, "Leave everything! Just do it!"

Now, they all caught sight of it, and although in shock, they did not panic, and for once, obeyed him.

*The Black Square* was furious. They had seen it! It launched itself at the car, as it moved away. It despised the Vilal, just as it despised everything else. At least though, they had given it the extra strength it lusted for. Without them though, it just did not have the speed. It tried but it could not catch them, not in the machine they drove in. They would have been so juicy as well, it thought.

For a long time after that, it wandered, trying to sense a fresh target. There was nothing though. The schools were abandoned. Even the houses and the shops. Where had all the people gone. For the first time since it had been here, it felt its shell weaken, the surface getting more brittle through lack of food. It did not want to feel the same as it did on its home world ever again. That consuming sense of hunger. Gnawing at it, sending it insane.

Then it caught a scent, something exotic. Could it be another trap? That hardly mattered now though, it had to feed, so it would risk it. It moved towards the new prey with. Evil excitement and a glee at the thought of fresh suffering gave it new strength.

Rick could not understand what had happened. One minute he was being held up as a savior, the darling of the local media. Even the world media was catching on, and he was set to become the phenomena that he had always believed would be his destiny. The healer of sick children! Then, Ian had died, had a heart attack allegedly, and his machine had been stolen. Rick did not believe that Ian had had a heart attack. He suspected that he had been murdered by the government. It was too much of a coincidence. Especially as the machine he had created had been stolen at the same time.

He had tried to tell them, but with these strange creatures running around, the media had moved on. He was unable to heal anymore, so Rick's story was now old news and not credible. He would be written off a flash in the pan, just another charlatan who got a bit lucky. Some of his followers had said that these evil creatures might be in some way connected with his healing powers, but he dismissed that as nonsense, and exiled them from his presence. He had tried to build another machine, but it had not worked. Most of his followers had now left. The hardcore remained though, and he still had the ranch, and millions left in the bank, so he would never have to work again.

Now, he sat in his new specially commissioned purple robes, trying to build another machine like Ian's. While the first one had not worked, he and his remaining followers would carry on trying though....

*The Black Square* was nearly there now, it could almost taste them. It rushed through the gateway to the stadium. Then it saw them, a man and a woman. Standing there. They would not taste as good as a child, that was for sure, but they would do, they would give it strength. It scanned the horizon for other humans. Their bullets could not penetrate its fabric, but it was worth looking.

Satisfied that the stadium was otherwise empty, it rushed towards them, ready to savor the kill. If they had guns, and it suspected they did, it would still be able to kill them easily, without enduring a single scratch. Bullets were no match for it.

"Your hunger has made you careless," said Jake out loud as he saw it move towards him and Charlotte.

It was now focused totally on the kill. So focused that it didn't hear the drone coming in behind it. And when the drone penetrated its skin, it didn't realize it had been destroyed and had exploded. Its consciousness was so evil and driven; it still willed itself along for a few seconds after its physicality had been terminated. The last thought of *The Black Square* was one of anger…

## *After...*

The King was delighted with the destruction of *The Black Square*. In fact, so delighted that he granted Jake a rare privilege. He was allowed to travel regularly between the human world and the Fairy Kingdom. The first human to be granted such a privilege in centuries. Mr. Saunders and Mr. McGee were also similarly delighted. They offered Charlotte a new identity should she wish to remain in the human world. Which she accepted, just in case she might find a permanent use for it. Jake and Charlotte ended up in a relationship. They were now regular and welcome attendees at the King's sumptuous and exquisite banquets in the Castle, and Jake became quite an accomplished dancer. Although, at the time of writing, it is just far too early to say whether they will live happily ever after or not.

Fortunately though, Rick and the Vilal were both rendered powerless.

At least for now.


## THE END

Made in United States
North Haven, CT
17 July 2022